FIT

KINDRED #2

USAT Bestselling Author

LIZZIE JAMES

Published by Lizzie James 2022
Edited by Eleanor Lloyd-Jones at Shower of Schmidt Designs
Formatted by Phoenix Book Designs
Cover Design by Lee Taylor at Coffin Print Designs

ONE
Sammy

It was just another boring Sunday, sitting in the lounge, staring out the window when I should have been focusing on the essay in front of me—the essay that I was slowly failing on; the essay that was also becoming the reason why I would never make it onto the pitch.

Football was my passion; it had been ever since I was old enough to kick a ball. It was all I'd ever wanted to do. When our father died, football became an escape for Johnny and me. Watching him progress through the ranks made me realize that this was possible—that playing this game professionally could be more than just a dream.

I knew that Johnny was going to make it to the

Professional leagues. He was going to become one of those names that people would chant in the stadiums throughout America. Maybe I'd follow him; maybe I wouldn't, but right now, it would be a fun ride just being a part of his team.

I was taken out of my thoughts when Tillie began waving her hand in front of my face.

"Earth to Sammy!" She was grinning down at me with a sparkle in her eyes. "You zoned out there."

I rolled my eyes at her teasing. Since Tillie moved in with us three months ago, she had slowly started to come out of her shell more. She was still a quiet person, but she had become more confident around us. She was just another member of the family.

"I was just talking to Joy on the phone. She'd like us over for dinner tonight." She phrased it like a question but we both knew it was a given. We never missed dinner at Joy's, even before Tillie moved here.

I nodded my head, giving her a small smile. "I'll be there."

She returned my smile before turning around and disappearing back upstairs. The sound of her high-pitched laughter soon filtered down.

I rolled my eyes. It could be really nauseating living with a blissfully in-love couple. I couldn't complain too much, though. Especially when I saw how happy she made my brother. Her laughter faded into silence before the slam of their bedroom door echoed.

That was my cue. I tried not to be in the house if they were having their own quiet time. Hearing my future sister in law scream my brother's name out in pleasure wasn't exactly on my list of things to do. I grabbed my jacket and keys and left the house, leaving them to it.

My feet took me in the direction of the coffee shop on the corner block. I grinned as I spotted Logan and Bex sitting at a table in the back. Walking over to them, I chuckled when I saw Logan reach over and pinch a bit of Bex's cookie off her plate. She smacked his hand lightly but laughed when he gave her a cheeky wink.

"What are you losers doing?"

Logan shuffled over a seat closer to Bex, offering his seat to me. "I thought you had to stick close to the house to get your essays done." He cocked an eyebrow at me, waiting for an answer.

"I was, but Johnny and Tillie were home." I raised my eyebrows suggestively, getting my hint across.

Logan laughed, tossing his head back.

"What's so funny?" Bex asked. She brought the cup to her lips, sipping her hot chocolate.

"Sammy here cringes at the thought of hearing

Tillie in the throes of passion." He had a mocking tone that just made Bex giggle.

I rolled my eyes at his teasing nature before grabbing a passing waiter's attention. I quickly ordered a black coffee.

"I wouldn't mind listening to Tillie make those noises..." Logan chimed in. He had a devious grin on his face.

I knew he was joking but he was only saying it to wind Bex up. Logan was the biggest prankster that I knew. If he wasn't winding someone up, he was plotting ways to wind someone up.

"Well, I will have to leave you two geeks." He stood up, squeezing past me and sliding his jacket on.

"Where are you going?" Bex asked. "Do you have a hot date?" She cocked her eyebrow in what I would normally assume to be a flirtatious way but then I remembered that men were never on Bex's radar. She was a lesbian and she was open about it.

My eyes narrowed in on Logan when I saw a very faint blush steel over his cheeks. That was new. Logan never blushed. I didn't think he knew how to blush.

Did he have a thing for Bex? Or did he have a hot date?

"The ladies are going to have to wait." He gave her a teasing wink before continuing. "I have a meeting with the coach to discuss my units regarding the medical credits for my course." He shrugged his shoulders. "Will see what happens. Catch you later, geeks." He gave us a quick wave before he was disappearing out the door.

"So, how are things with Bex?"

She smiled at me before grabbing her sketch pad from her bag. "I've been trying to focus more on landscapes." She flipped it open before turning it for me to inspect. "What do you think?"

"Well, I can see where you're trying."

"You jerk!" She snatched her sketch pad back, hiding it from my view.

We both laughed at my teasing. She knew she was an amazing artist. I don't know why she felt she needed the verbal confirmation. She wasn't as good at drawing landscapes as Tillie but then again, Tillie wasn't as good at animations as she was.

"So, what are you doing tonight?" she asked, changing the subject.

"We're over at Joy's tonight. You're not coming?"

She shook her head, negatively. "I have a date tonight." She gave me a sexy wink that gave me shivers.

I couldn't deny it. Bex was a very good looking girl and one I wouldn't mind getting to know better. As far as I knew though, she was only into girls. Although, she had often gotten a bit closer to me when we had both had a few drinks. Maybe she swung both ways?

"Where did you disappear to?" She giggled before biting her delectable bottom lip. "Did I lose you to some hot lesbian fantasies about me?"

Fuck, this girl was trouble.

"Maybe." I grinned over at her, loving the giggle that came from her.

The smile on her face slowly vanished. She grabbed her jacket and slipped the sketch pad back into her bag.

"I have to get going as well. I need to go to the library before going back to the dorms to get ready for tonight." She stood, giving me a quick kiss on the cheek before disappearing out the door.

I sat there for a few moments longer, slowly finishing my coffee. Looking at my watch, I saw I had been out of the house for over an hour. That should have been enough time.

I quickly stood, cringing when I bumped into a solid body. "I'm so sorry," I quickly apologized.

"That's okay, Sammy," a deep, masculine voice replied.

I looked up, meeting a pair of striking green eyes. "Uh..."

"It is Sammy, right?" He grinned at me. "You play on the college football team?"

I nodded, dumbfounded. Why was this guy looking at me like this? Was he…?

When Tillie first arrived in town, she and I had hung out several times at the skate park; which is where I had first seen this guy. He was usually there teaching the young skaters how to stand on their boards and dismount properly—not sure why as he didn't exactly look like a saint. He had a devious glint in his eye and had plagued my mind since I first saw him.

Which was really messed up.

I'd had several girlfriends in high school and I'd spent more than a few nights in a few of the sorority sisters' beds since arriving here, but it was no secret that I could silently admit to myself that I had been struggling the last few weeks since arriving here and seeing this man in front of me more than a few times had stirred something new in me.

I thought I was straight. I had always acted straight. My sexuality had never been a problem but now, the man that plagued my thoughts was standing in front of me making me question everything. He smiled at me, making his face gentler. "I'm sorry." He shook his head, extending his arm to me. "I'm Benjamin."

"Sammy." I smiled back, shaking his hand. A

shiver raced down my spine at the contact, making me freeze. I looked around subtly—or at the very least I meant for it to be subtle—before his fingers tightened around my hand. "It's okay." He had a soothing lilt to his tone.

I frowned at him.

Okay? This wasn't okay! Nothing about this was okay.

"Sammy, I understand." He released my hand before tucking his hands into his jean pockets. "I know things are difficult for you at the moment."

I frowned, even more confused. "Are you...?"

He nodded. "I'm not asking for anything, Sammy. I would just like to get to know you more."

"Uh, I'm not sure." I took a step back from him, scared and excited all at once. I wanted what he was offering but I was scared to accept it. Scared of things changing. I wasn't ready for that kind of change.

"Think it over." His eyes flicked past me before coming back to mine. "I work at Wicked Ink a few shops up." He nodded his head towards the door to emphasize his point. "Look me up if you ever want to talk." He gave me a tense smile and left me standing there.

I followed after him a few moments later, feeling worse than when I arrived. I guess I hadn't been very subtle over the last few months. I guess that every time I'd been watching him, he'd been watching me as well.

I went straight home and disappeared into my room. Right now, I just wanted to disappear from my thoughts for a while. Maybe the dinner at Joy's tonight would help—give me some time to shut down.

A few hours later, we were crossing the road to Joy's and being welcomed into her home. She was so excited to see us as she always was. Tillie followed her into the kitchen and began helping to carry the trays of lasagne and salad into the dining room.

"And here's Sammy's," Joy said, carrying a smaller dish of tofu lasagne in.

"Thank you, Joy." She fussed over each of the boys before giving me a quick kiss on the cheek and smoothing the hair back from my forehead. "How are you doing Sammy?" She placed her hand over mine, squeezing gently. "How is football going?"

The table went silent.

Ever since Lucy went psychotic on Johnny and Tillie, Joy had gone super protective of me. I think it really shook her.

"I'm not sure yet." I gave her a smile, trying to make them all feel better. "I'm still training every day." I cleared my throat, needing to be okay with this part. "I mean, yeah, there's a chance I may not be able to play again, but..." I shrugged my shoulders before looking at Tillie. "I wouldn't change it."

Tillie smiled widely at me, showing off her pearly white teeth. Johnny pulled her hand to his lips, pressing a kiss to her knuckles. We all knew how lucky we were to have them both sitting there. If losing football was the price, then I'd happily take it. Tillie had become the glue in our house and she was already family to me.

We slowly finished dinner and I was thoroughly stuffed. Watching Tillie and Johnny caused my mind to drift back to Benjamin. He seemed to understand how I was feeling and what I was thinking. He seemed to understand that I had no clue what direction I should go.

I shook my head to clear it when Joy began gently tapping my hand. She gave me a big smile, not laughing like the rest of the table was.

"You zoned out again," Tillie teased, giving me a cheeky wink.

"Just thinking." I grinned, rolling my eyes at their teasing nature.

"He's been doing that a lot lately," Johnny chimed in. "I think Sammy here has gotten a girl." He winked at Tillie.

I rolled my eyes at them. If only they knew.

"Well she must be a lucky girl, if that's true," Joy chimed in, giving me a sweet smile.

"Just a friend at the moment." I smiled back at her, trying to ignore Johnny's, Tillie's and Logan's stares.

"You can never have too many friends," Tillie chimed in. She entwined her hand with Johnny's and rested it on the table. "You never know what else it can lead to."

I smiled in return before looking back to Joy.

"Thank you for dinner, Joy."

Everyone else chimed in with their thanks and before I knew it, they were all getting ready to leave.

"Ready for me to kick your ass at FIFA?" Logan asked, nodding his head towards the Xbox.

I rolled my eyes. He always kicked my ass at FIFA and he knew it.

"Uh..." My eyes flicked between him and Joy where she was hugging Tillie. "If it's okay, I was hoping to hang out here with Joy for a little longer?" I phrased it as a question, suddenly unsure. I knew I was always welcome here at Joy's but I just... I needed someone to talk to that wasn't family.

"Of course, my dear." Joy turned her kind gaze on me, smiling sweetly.

Tillie turned to look at Johnny with a confused

expression on her face. He shrugged his shoulders, obviously not understanding either.

"I'll catch up with you guys later." I gave them a tense smile.

They quickly said their goodbyes to Joy and made their way back across the street.

I took a seat on the sofa in her lounge and waited for Joy to join me. What the fuck was I doing? I wasn't ready for this but I... I just couldn't stop it happening.

I liked girls. But lately... I also liked boys. I shook my head. No, not boys. One boy. Just one in particular.

"Sweetie..." Joy took a seat next to me and placed her hand on my shoulder. "Is everything okay? You look like you have the weight of the world on your shoulders."

She looked so concerned. I hated worrying her, but I needed to talk to someone.

"Is this about the young girl that Johnny mentioned?" She cocked an eyebrow at me, looking patient.

"Um, kind of?" I cleared my throat, trying to get rid of my nerves. "I've met someone and I... I don't know what to do..."

"What do you mean?" She took my hand in hers

and rested it on my leg. "Are you not looking for a relationship?"

"It's not that." I shook my head. Finding the words to explain to Joy was difficult. If I couldn't tell Joy, how the hell was I going to even tell my own family what was happening?

"You can talk to me, sweetheart." She gave me a warm smile, squeezing my hand in her clasped hands.

"I met someone."

She opened her mouth but before she could say anything, I quickly continued.

"His name is Benjamin."

Her eyes widened before her mouth dropped open.

I cringed at her reaction, waiting for her to start shouting. "It's bad, right?"

I began to pull my hand from hers, but her grip tightened.

"Sweetheart, no, of course not."

She shook her head, shuffling closer to me. She wrapped her arms around me and squeezed me closer to her.

I went willingly, appreciating the hug more than anything.

She pressed a small kiss to my forehead before moving the hair back off my forehead.

"I'm so proud of you."

"Proud?" I asked with disgust. "Proud of me for being different?"

"You are not different!" she demanded. "If you have met someone that can be your missing piece, the way that Tillie and Johnny are each other's missing pieces, then yes, my sweet boy. I am proud."

I tilted my head up, needing to see her face. "You think so?"

"Of course." She rested her head on top of mine, rubbing my upper arm.

"So, what do I do now?" I was so lost. I had no clue what I was supposed to do.

"Get to know this Benjamin. Remember what Tillie said about friends?"

"You never know what they can lead to," I whispered, repeating her words from dinner.

"Exactly. You need to stop stressing, Sammy."

I nodded, feeling marginally better than I thought I would after telling someone my deep, dark secret.

"Just focus on yourself for now. Get to know Benjamin and all will fall into place. I promise."

TWO
Benjamin

Fourteen weeks and two days.

That is how long I had been obsessed with that man. Sammy. Today was the day. I couldn't take just watching him from across the skate park any longer.

I knew he was interested in me. Well, I was ninety-nine percent sure he was interested in me. Two guys didn't just stare and make lustful eyes at each other for fun, right?

At first, I thought he was straight as he was always with the same girl every time but then, when he left her with that bigger guy in the park that day, I knew for a definite that they were unattached.

Since then, we saw each other a few times a week at

the park. He was usually with that girl and was either watching her sketch, looking across at me teaching the kids how to ride their boards or doodling on his own bit of paper.

It didn't take a genius to figure it out.

When I first approached him in the coffee shop, I was surprised at the surge of emotions that went through me from one touch. I expected to only lust after Sammy. I didn't expect to be hit by such strong, protective feelings.

He looked scared.

I don't know why I assumed that he was already out of the closet. He wasn't. Far from it. He was probably wedged in that closet and by the look of worry that was on his face, he had no intention of coming out of it anytime soon.

I could relate to that. When I came out to my parents, my old man kicked my ass so hard, I was still hobbling on one leg the next day. Not my best moment.

I didn't want that for Sammy. Fuck, I wouldn't want that for anyone.

I soon moved out after that and came here.

Not long after moving, I got a job in the local tattoo shop and haven't looked back since. I've been with a few men, but nothing has been serious. I didn't think I really believed in serious relationships.

Honestly, I'd never had much of an example of a serious committed relationship that lasted.

But there was something about Sammy. With him, I was willing to give it a try...

Walking into Wicked Ink, I groaned at the knotted muscles that were aching in my shoulders. Spending the rest of the night being hunched over my tattoo gun wasn't exactly what I needed.

"How did it go?" Lily asked, sounding way too fucking excited for any sane person to be. She knew all about my fascination with Sammy and came with me to all his games.

Football wasn't exactly my most favorite sport to watch, but it was really the only place where I could see Sammy. It's not like I was stalking him or anything, but I wasn't exactly the kind of guy that just strutted up to a guy and declare myself to them.

Declare myself. Fuck, I sounded like some 18th century poet.

I shook my head negatively and the smile dropped from her face.

She knew without me even having to say anything. "He's not ready."

"I don't think so." I hung my jacket up and

approached the reception counter. "I told him to come find me if he ever needs someone to talk to."

She understood where I was coming from. Lily was a lesbian and she knew better than anyone how life changing this decision could be. She patted me on the shoulder as I walked to my station, ready to start my shift.

We were both kept busy. I had a few small art designs to do on a few college students and Lily always had a customer with her for an eyebrow bar or belly ring appointment. Our shop was usually busy. Lily and I worked there on a rotating basis. That week we were doing the evening shift and Darren and Tyler were working the day shift. We'd usually swap the following week and cover each other when needed. Tyler and Lily owned the shop, but they never made any decisions without asking mine and Darren's viewpoint.

I was lucky. I had found my own little family here and I was more appreciative of that then they knew. I just hoped Sammy had the same.

The days slowly passed into weeks and Sammy never came. Maybe I had read the situation wrongly. Maybe he just stared at people.

Fuck, I was such an idiot. He must have thought I was a complete weirdo.

I focused back on the customer in front of me. I

was adding the finishing touches to the pin-up impression of his wife on his left arm. She had passed away a few years back, but he wanted her with him always. It was sweet in a morbid kind of way.

Just as I was finishing up and wrapping some film around his arm, Lily called my name.

"You have a visitor, Ben." She gave me a small smile before her eyes focused on my customer. "I can take care of the rest if you'd like?"

"Sure." I nodded, shaking his hand quickly and sent him out the door with Lily. She was already chattering away to him like they were best friends.

I turned away to wipe my hands when I heard a pair of footsteps coming in my direction.

I turned around, surprised when I saw Sammy stood there, looking completely lost. He slowly slipped his hands into his jean pockets and rocked back and forth on his heels.

"H-hi," I stuttered, like a geeky pre-teen.

I had given up hoping he'd come. After the first few days of waiting, I had become like some obsessed stalker constantly looking out the windows of the shop. It had been a pathetic sight.

"Hi." He gave me a small smile before continuing. "I know it's been a while."

I nodded, not knowing what to say. I needed him

to lead me in this, otherwise, I'd only fuck it up and send him running in the other direction. I didn't want him running that way. I knew we didn't know each other but I wanted him to run to me. Not away from me.

More than anything, I wanted to be there to help him.

"I thought about what you said to me—about wanting to get to know me?" He sounded so unsure.

It was right then I realized just how confused and frustrated he must be. If I could help him learn from my mistakes, I'd do whatever it took. People didn't have any clue how hard this decision of sexuality could be on a person's health. It drained you physically and mentally until you didn't know which way was up.

"I'd like to get to know you. I know we don't really know much about each other but..."

What else could I say? 'I've been thinking about you non-stop since laying eyes on you and I want so much more than to just get to know you, but I don't want to scare you away'? Yeah, I was sure that would go down great.

"If you want to that is?" Now I sounded like the unsure one. I mentally rolled my eyes at myself. "Maybe we could grab a drink after work one night?"

My breath froze in my chest at the blinding smile that graced his face.

Fuck, I was so screwed.

"I'd like that," he enthused. "Are you free tonight?"

Fuck! I hadn't expected that.

Before I could answer, Lily appeared behind him, peeking her head around Sammy.

"He's free." She had a devious smile on her face, but it softened as Sammy turned to look down at her. She barely came up to his shoulder; she was like a fairy standing next to him.

He introduced himself, offering his hand to her. "I'm Sammy."

"I'm Lily." She grinned back at him, shaking his hand. "I like you. You're cute!"

I chuckled at how honest she was. That was one of the things I loved about Lily. If she thought it, she said it. It was just the way that she was.

"What about my appointments?" I asked, quickly butting in. I could already see a faint pink blush coloring the backs of Sammy's ears.

"We don't have any. Our last appointment just called to re-arrange so we may as well close early." She smiled sweetly at me but she forgot how well I really knew her. I wouldn't have put it past her if she'd rung them to rearrange just to get us out the door.

"We're going to go for a drink," Sammy chimed in. "Do you want to come with us?"

Her eyes flicked to me and I gave her a small nod. I didn't mind if Lily joined us, especially if it made Sammy more comfortable.

"Sure!" she agreed enthusiastically. "I'd love to. Let me just close up the till and I'll be with you."

"Is that okay?" Sammy asked, turning back to me. "That she...?"

"Of course, it is." I smiled back at him. "I don't mind sharing you."

His eyes widened at my statement and I wanted to slap myself. There I was, supposed to be making him comfortable with me and I was fucking hitting on him.

I grabbed my coat from behind Lily and glared at her as I caught her cheeky smile. She was not helping.

Being Sammy's friend was going to be a lot harder than I thought. Pun intended.

We made our way outside and while I quickly locked up, I chuckled silently as I saw Lily make her way behind Sammy to check him out. She looked impressed when her eyes landed on his ass. We began making our way up the block to Joey's Bar when Lily slipped in between us and linked her arm with Sammy's.

"So, Sammy, where do you work?" Her inquisitive

eyes gazed up at him as she pasted a big smile on her face.

He grinned down at her, looking a lot more comfortable than when he'd first entered the shop.

I leaned my hand down and gently squeezed her fingers, thanking her silently. Having Lily join us made it less of a date and more just three friends hanging out.

"I'm in college."

"And what are you studying?" She knew all these details due to my obsessive window watching tendencies, but it didn't stop her. She was like my own little secret weapon.

"I'm studying management and finance but I'm also a reserve on the football team."

His face fell when he mentioned football. It confused me, and from the side glance Lily cast me, I wasn't the only one puzzled by his statement.

We quickly entered the pub and picked a table at the back of the room. It looked busy, but the noise wasn't deafening. We ordered a couple beers for myself and Lily and Sammy ordered a shandy.

"Not much of a drinker?" I asked, curious. Most guys his age would be knocking them back.

He shook his head negatively, shrugging off his jacket. "I try not to drink loads. I try to stay in shape."

Lily cocked her eyebrow, probably thinking he was bullshitting us.

He chuckled. "I mean, yeah, I drink if I'm at a party or something, but I'm only a reserve on the team and I'm dying to get up there and play an actual game. So..." He shrugged his shoulders, dismissively. "I try to pass on the drink offers where I can."

"Fair enough." She shrugged her shoulders. "It sounds very boring. I'm glad I'm not a footballer."

We both laughed at her pouting face. She would never make it on a strict diet regime. She loved donuts too much.

"So, what made you become a piercist?" Sammy asked, directing his question to Lily.

"Want to know a secret?" She grinned at him, shuffling closer. "I like causing pain."

Sammy's eyes widened in surprise before they both burst out laughing. She looked like an adult version of Tinkerbell and here she was acting like a sadist.

"I'm actually part owner as well." She had a proud smile on her face.

"Oh, wow, that's amazing!" Sammy enthused.

"I run it with my twin brother, Tyler. Our parents died when we were eighteen and we used our inheritance to open up shop." She sounded upbeat, but I knew how much she missed her mother. They never worked the anniversary of their death. They both disappeared and they never talked about it.

Over the next hour, Lily tried to get Sammy to explain the rules of football to her but it was falling on deaf ears. She looked more confused than when he'd started. A few minutes later, she shook her head and held her hands up in defeat, stopping the conversation.

"Forget I asked." She giggled. "I will just continue being blissfully ignorant and carry on admiring the player's butts." She tossed the last of her drink back and stood.

"That's it for me. I will have to leave you boys to it." She slipped her jacket on and turned to Sammy. "Give me a hug."

He stood up, wrapping her tiny frame in a bear hug. "It was lovely meeting you, Lily."

"You too, sugar." She gave him a kiss on the cheek before doing the same with me. "Call me when you get home."

"Yes, boss."

She giggled, giving us a small wave and leaving us to it.

"Lily seems really nice," Sammy complimented.

I chuckled, secretly loving his words. "More like bossy." I grinned at him, liking how his face lit up.

"Well, technically she is the boss." He grinned at me, taking a sip of his drink.

"Touché." I chuckled, finishing the last of my drink.

I ordered another shandy and a coke, not wanting tonight to be affected by an alcoholic buzz.

"So, Sammy…" I started, needing some answers now that it was just the two of us. "I was starting to think I had said the wrong thing to you at the coffee shop."

He glanced away from me, avoiding my eyes. "Is that why you haven't been to the skate park lately?"

"A little, yeah." I looked back at him, loving how green his eyes were. "Did you go to the skate park hoping I'd be there?"

"A little, yeah." We both chuckled at his words.

"We make a good pair, don't we?" I joked.

"Have you… Do you…?" He cleared his throat, fidgeting in his seat. "Do your friends know that you're gay?"

"Yeah." I nodded my head. "I came out to my family two years ago and it didn't go great."

"What happened?" he asked, eagerly.

"My father kicked the crap out of me."

He cringed at my words and I hated causing that reaction in him.

"I walked out of the house a few days later and I never went back."

"That must have been hard for you." He was trying to comfort me but it no longer affected me.

Lily had taught me that if people couldn't love you for who you were, then they didn't deserve a place in your life. It was a hard lesson to learn but I was better off for it.

"So, how long have you been...?" I was inquisitive. I needed him to be as open with me as I was being with him.

"I'm not gay," he defended, shaking his head. "I'm just..." His shoulders slumped in defeat. "I'm just not straight, either."

I nodded my head, understanding his statement.

"I've been with girls, but..." He stared into my eyes.

"But what?" I whispered, tightening my grip on my glass.

"But it feels different." His hand tensed on the table. "With you. It feels different."

"I want it to be different, Sammy." I leaned my hand across the table and held it open to him, resting it palm up. I wanted him to put his hand in mine but he never did.

His shoulders slumped and he pulled his hands

closer to his body. His eyes darted around behind me, a look of worry in his eyes.

"I'm sorry... I can't..." He shook his head, looking as lost as he had done in that coffee shop weeks ago.

"Don't be sorry." I shook my head. I pulled my hand back and placed it back around my glass. "It's understandable."

Understandable and completely fucking shit.

THREE
Sammy

I hated pulling my hand away. I'd wanted to take his hand—I'd wanted to take it, accept what he was offering and never look back. I just hadn't been able to. Talking about our situation and living it were two entirely different things. What if he rejected me? What if I wasn't enough?

"I should get going," I said, my eyes flicking to the door.

Benjamin nodded, standing up. He didn't even attempt to finish his coke. Maybe he was eager for me to leave? Maybe he realised that this was more head-work than he wanted to sign up for.

I walked past him, feeling that eagerness start to flow into me now. I inhaled him as I passed him, loving the peppermint smell that wafted from him. He was perfect without even trying. He was kind, compassionate, patient, caring... He ticked every damn box.

We began walking in the direction of my house which made me eager to know where he lived. Did he live close by? Is that why he was often at the skate park? Was he always there because he knew the kids? Or was it something else?

He chuckled next to me, taking my attention. "What has you thinking so hard?" He grinned at me, making me smile back in return.

"Just wondering where you live?" I grinned.

"I live at the end of this street." He pointed straight ahead, indicating the block of apartments at the end. They looked nice from the outside.

"I live a block away." I pointed across the road to the right. I was surprised how close we lived to each other.

He nodded. "I enjoyed tonight."

"You did?" I was shocked. He sure didn't look like he had enjoyed it.

"I did. I like spending time with you, Sammy." He cocked his head to the side before continuing. "I mean, I know we're in different places in our lives and all..."

I nodded, not sure what to say in response.

"But I..." He cleared his throat, coming to a stop. "I'm here if you ever need anything."

He wanted to say more. I know that he did but he didn't. He just stood there, staring at me.

Was he waiting for me to make the first move? Was I waiting for him to make the first move to kiss me—to show me how different it could be from the girls? There was obviously something there... I just wasn't sure if I was ready to find out what it was.

I gave an awkward wave and made my way across the street. I was acting like some prissy pre-teen version of myself. I mean, so what if I was into boys? It's not like it made me a different person. Right?

I shook my head, making my way inside a dark house. I went into the kitchen and poured a glass of milk, stealing a quick cookie, and made my way up the stairs.

After speaking to Joy about Benjamin several weeks ago, I'd been determined to go and see him right away—determined and very scared. I wasn't ready for some big life-changing decision. I had enough of those going on right now with football. I had one more month of rehabilitation and if my arm didn't fully recover, then I would be removed from the team.

If that day came, I wasn't sure how I would handle it, but I would never regret my actions. What happened with Tillie was the most natural and honest thing I had ever done for another. My family would be there a lot longer than football. A life without football would be a lot easier to handle than a life without Tillie.

The next day, after many hours of marketing strategies and acronyms that just fried my brain, I was about to leave the house when there was a knock at the door. I never expected it to be Benjamin standing on my doorstep.

"Hi." I couldn't hide the surprise in my tone.

I was half expecting that, after my awkwardness from the previous night, I wouldn't be seeing him again so soon.

"Can I come in?" His eyes moved past me before coming back to rest on mine.

"I'm actually just leaving for class. Do you want to walk with me instead?"

"Yes." He breathed a sigh of relief, taking a step back from the doorway.

I grabbed my bag and joined him outside, giving him a small smile.

After a few minutes of silence, he heaved a sigh of what sounded like frustration. "I wanted to apologize for last night."

I frowned in confusion. What did he have to be

sorry for? I'd been the awkward one. If anyone needed to apologize, it was me.

"For what?" I asked, voicing my concerns.

"You're in a confused place at the moment." He slid his hands into his jean pockets before continuing. "I know how difficult that is and I... I don't want you to feel like I'm not understanding." He flicked his gaze to me before looking away again. "Telling you my experience last night wasn't fair to you. My father was a mean bastard and I don't want what happened to me to affect your situation."

I nodded my head, not even thinking that. I couldn't lie: I was scared to tell Johnny, but I wasn't afraid that he would react violently. Johnny would never hurt me. Well, maybe if I made a move on Tillie, but that would never happen. I silently chuckled at the thought.

We turned the corner and my marketing building came into view. He was silent for the next few moments before he placed his hand on my upper arm and pulled me to a stop.

"I told you all the negative stuff that can happen when a person makes this decision. That was wrong." He shook his head before a bright smile covered his face. "I should have started with the good things."

Shivers traveled down my arm from his touch before he slowly removed his hand.

"What are you doing tonight?" He kicked the toe of his shoe against the ground. "Lily has asked us to go out with her tonight. It's not a date. I just want to show you how non-scary this decision can be."

I narrowed my eyes, thinking over his question. Not a date.

My eyes trailed over his face, over his square jaw, the slight stubble on his face, his deep, green eyes. He was very good looking but it wasn't just those qualities that had drawn me to him. I believed it was his good character. How sweet, gentle and patient he was being.

"Come out with us tonight and meet my family. The family that I run Wicked Ink with." The most dazzling smile slowly stretched across his face. "If you enjoy it, maybe we can go from there."

I nodded my head slowly. "Okay."

His eyes brightened at my agreement.

"That sounds like fun." I grinned at him before turning away and walking towards my class.

I took a sneaky look over my shoulder and chuckled when I saw he was still standing there, watching me walk away. As I turned back around, I collided straight into Bex.

"Who's the hottie?" she asked, looking over my shoulder.

I laughed at her choice of words. "Benjamin. He works at Wicked Ink."

Her eyebrows rose at my words before a small giggle escaped her. "Does he now?"

Why was she looking at me with the biggest grin on her face? Did she know? Fuck she knew.

"See you later, Sammy." She gave me a wink before she left me to it, jogging across the quad to her own class.

The end of the day arrived slowly, but when it did, I left campus and hurried toward home

"Hey!" Logan greeted me. "You out tonight? The Greeks are partying tonight and you and I, my friend, have been invited out." He had a devious grin on his face.

"I have plans, I'm sorry." I cringed at my reply. He would now have questions.

"Anyone I know?" He smirked, naturally assuming that it was a girl.

"Uh, I don't think so." Before he could interrupt, I quickly continued. "Listen, man, I've got to go." I clapped my hand against his shoulder before starting my jog home.

I refused to worry or panic about the crazy mess that had become my life. All I was going to do was focus on tonight and whatever it was that Benjamin wanted to show me.

Walking into the house, I could see Johnny and Tillie cuddling in the lounge. I had every plan to ignore them and just go straight upstairs but Tillie stopped me.

"Hey, Sammy! How was school?"

I couldn't ignore her. "It was good. Marketing is kicking my ass but I hear that's normal." I chuckled, causing her to smile.

"I hear you have a date tonight," she continued.

I swear her and Logan were like two gossip queens.

"Not a date," I denied. "Just out with a friend."

"Anyone we know?" Johnny asked, interrupting. They both smirked at me, making me just wish that the ground would swallow me up.

"No." I shook my head, placing my bag down by the end of the sofa. "Now, if all the questions are over, I'm going to go and have a shower." I chuckled as I climbed the stairs, eager to get away from their questions.

Since the shooting with Lucy, Johnny had become

very protective; not only of Tillie but me as well. He'd always been protective of Tillie but what happened had really shaken him. Johnny had always been very easy going but what he went through left him scarred.

We all were, really.

An hour later, I was showered, shaved and just fastening up my blue checked shirt when there was a knock at the door. A shot of panic coursed through me when I realized that Benjamin would now be meeting some of *my* family.

I sat down on the end of my bed, taking a deep breath to attempt to calm my nerves.

Don't freak out, don't freak out.

Taking a final deep breath, I slid my sneakers on and made my way down the stairs.

Walking into the lounge, I breathed a sigh of relief when I saw that it was only Tillie here. Johnny must have gone for a run.

Tillie was standing by the fireplace and Benjamin and Lily were sitting on the sofa, looking right at home. Well, Lily looked right at home; Benjamin looked kind of uncomfortable.

"So, where are you guys going?" Tillie asked, ever inquisitive.

"We're meeting up with some friends of mine just outside of town," Lily said, standing up.

Benjamin stood with her, and seeing their outfits, I was glad I was dressed in a similarly casual way. I trailed my eyes down Benjamin's solid build and quickly shot them to Tillie. Her gaze turned to Benjamin before recognition dawned in her eyes.

"Do I know you?" she asked, frowning.

"Yes." He nodded. "I think we've seen each other a few times at the skate park?" He smiled pleasantly at her, waiting for her to agree.

Her eyes flicked between Benjamin and me for a few moments before she nodded, giving him a pleasant smile. She walked past us, leading everyone to the main door. "Well, have fun, guys!"

Benjamin and Lily led the way from the house.

Just as I went to follow, Tillie grabbed my hand, entwining our fingers.

"Sammy," she whispered, rubbing her thumb over the pulse on my wrist. "Have fun, okay?"

I frowned, curiously. Did she know? Had she caught on? When she realized just who Benjamin was, had it all added up? She wasn't a stupid girl and whenever she went to the skate park, I'd always tag along.

"You've been so serious lately." She rubbed her palm over my cheek. "You deserve to be happy. Just like the rest of us."

She knew. Even if she didn't know, she knew enough to suspect something.

I thought I would feel fear or panic at the thought of someone other than Joy knowing, but I didn't. I felt only acceptance and relief.

I brought her hand to my lips and pressed a quick kiss to her knuckles causing a beautiful smile to cover her face. I followed Lily to the car, getting in the back with her while Benjamin got in the passenger seat.

"Sammy, this is my other half, Trixie."

I smiled, giving her a friendly wave.

I'd had no clue that Lily was a lesbian but I was impressed at how openly honest she was. It was just another part of her I guess and a part that she seemed proud of.

"The boys are going to meet us there."

My gaze swung back to Lily and I smiled when I saw her looking at me.

"So where are you taking me?" I asked, intrigued.

"Only to the best place on earth," she replied.

Before I could ask, Benjamin turned his head and answered for her. "Bowling!" His grin was infectious and I immediately began to relax.

"I've never been bowling before," I admitted.

All three of them yelled at the same time, "Shut up!"

I laughed at their mock indignation.

"What kind of person hasn't been bowling before?" She looked insulted. "We are fixing that tonight," Lily declared, a look of determination crossing her face.

We slowly pulled into the parking spot outside the bowling place, and Lily was like a bottle of pop. She was bouncing in her seat, waiting for the car to stop.

"They'd better have pink shoes," she mumbled under her breath.

I chuckled at her and wondered what was so exciting about bowling.

As soon as I got out of the car, she grabbed my hand and began pulling me towards the doors. "Sammy's on our team!" she declared.

I laughed at her enthusiasm and loved how welcome she made me feel.

Benjamin chuckled at her eagerness, causing me to turn back to look at him.

He winked at me, making me feel things I hadn't felt with anyone.

Hope coursed through me making me feel that tonight would change things.

Hope that all would be okay—that, just like Benjamin said earlier today, good things can also happen.

FOUR
Benjamin

fter the girls promptly declared that Sammy
should be on their team to even up the
numbers, I basically lost him to their female clutches
for the next two hours. He must have been their lucky
charm as they promptly kicked our asses.

When Lily had suggested that we take Sammy
bowling, I'd had no clue what her angle was. Watching
him now, though, with Lily clinging to his back, I
knew that it had been the right decision.

I could talk about homosexual relationships with
Sammy until I was blue in the face, but actually being
around two homosexual relationships and demon-
strating to him that the world wouldn't end if Lily
kissed Trixie or if Darren slipped his hand into Tyler's

back jean pocket did more than anything verbally could have.

I wasn't trying to push Sammy into this life but I also didn't want him to make a decision that would be the safest option. I couldn't deny that I wanted Sammy to look at me the way that Lily looked at Trix.

The way that I wanted to look at him.

Sammy was vulnerable and sensitive, and I didn't want to ruin that. I wanted Sammy to be in this with me because he wanted to be in this with me. He plagued my thoughts day and night and I wanted him to be okay with himself before he could even think about being okay as an us.

He slid her down and took her pink bowling shoes off her, giving them back to the lady behind the counter. Walking over to the Italian restaurant across the street, I smiled to myself as Lily and Trixie linked arms with me. Sammy was currently comparing football statistics with Darren and Tyler. They were both big fans and they seemed to be getting along well.

"I really like him," Lily whispered to me, resting her head on my upper arm. "How are things?"

I shrugged, not knowing what to say. "I'm not really sure."

I waved them ahead while Sammy held the door open.

An hour later, we were exiting the restaurant, completely stuffed.

"That pizza was delicious!" Sammy enthused, rubbing his stomach.

I chuckled. My attention was quickly taken when Lily came skipping over to us with a deviously wicked grin spread across her face. "Trix and I are going to get a ride back with Tyler." She winked at me before turning to look at Sammy. "Do you want to come with us or are you okay having Ben drive you back?"

His eyes flickered briefly between Lily and I before he nodded. "Yeah, that's no problem."

I wanted to mock punch the air in celebration but I refused. It was best not to let my inner geek out just yet.

"See you later, boys." Lily turned away and began making her way over to where the rest of the group were waiting. "Don't do anything I wouldn't do," she called over her shoulder.

We both chuckled at her parting comment and began making our way over to the car.

"So, this is your car?" Sammy asked, gesturing to my blue Fiesta.

"It is. Trixie likes driving, though, so I let her drive when she wants to."

"Not every man would give his car to a girl to drive," he pointed out.

It was a very sexist comment to make but it didn't sound offensive coming from Sammy. He looked too inquisitive to be offensive. He was a lot like Lily in that way. I was finding that if he wanted to know something, he would just ask. It was an admirable quality.

"I'm not like every man." I smiled over at him, liking the honesty.

I had never really found someone that I could be brutally honest with before. It was a feeling that I was enjoying.

I pressed the button to automatically unlock the door and groaned in frustration when I saw Sammy's cheeks were turning pink. Normally, I would assume it was from the cold but considering the way he was avoiding my stare, I dared to hope it was lust.

Getting into the car, I smiled when Sammy immediately grabbed my iPod connected to the stereo and began scrolling through my playlists.

"You have so many songs on here!" He turned his infectious grin to me.

"I love music!" I defended. "You'll find songs from all genres in there."

I started the car and began the drive home. After a few moments, he finally decided on the band, Skillet.

They were my favorite band and I was secretly pleased that he appeared to like them as well.

My eyes trailed down when he ran his palm over his jean-clad leg, making me mentally groan.

Fuck! I had never been much of a leg man but with Sammy, any part of him looked good.

I turned my attention fully back to the road, seeing the junction for my street ahead. I pulled to a stop outside my place and turned my head, surprised when Sammy was already staring at me.

"Thanks for coming tonight."

"I had fun." His eyes trailed down to my chest before coming back to my eyes. "Thanks for inviting me."

Fuck, was he checking me out? I was sure it was the first time I'd ever seen Sammy look at me like that

I looked at the clock and noticed that it was only 9 pm. Still too early to end the night, right?

"Would you like to come in for a drink?" I asked. I was half hopeful and half nervous about what his answer was going to be. It was too soon.

"Sure." He nodded his head, smiling shyly at me.

Fuck. I hadn't been expecting that.

Getting out of the car, my hands shook as I got my keys out of my pocket. I rolled my eyes at myself, needing to chill the fuck out.

Leading him inside, we scaled three flights of stairs with Sammy behind me the whole way. I felt like some geeky teen going on his first date. My hands shook as I tried sliding the key into the lock.

"You okay?" Sammy asked, his sweet breath blowing across the back of my neck.

I nodded, steadying my hand. The key slid home and I walked through the door, flicking the lights on as I went.

"Come on in. Would you like a drink?" I turned to look at him and frowned when I saw him rubbing his hand against his right leg. The leg thing was definitely a nervous habit. It had to be. Maybe a drink would chill him out.

"Yeah, that'd be good." He smiled before turning to close the door.

"Make yourself at home." I walked to the kitchen and grabbed two bottles of beer from the fridge, popping the caps. "Do you want a glass?" I called before I entered the lounge.

Sammy was sitting on the sofa, looking over my worn copy of the Inked magazine.

"No, thanks." He didn't even look up, too engrossed in the designs on the printed page.

I placed his bottle on the coffee table in front of him and took a seat on the other end of the sofa, leaving a spot in between us. Sammy would have to set the pace.

Looking at him, I smiled at the way the little 'V' would deepen in between his brows when he was concentrating. He also had the sexiest pout on his face that I just wanted to kiss off. Before I could look away, his head shot up to look at me. He placed the magazine back on the table and lifted the bottle to his lips.

"Sorry about that." He chuckled before taking a long swig.

He looked so at peace sitting there. I could have stared at him all day.

"So, do you enjoy being a tattooist?"

"I love it," I enthused, turning my body sideways. "I'd always been artistic as a child but when it comes to marking people with my ink... I get the biggest buzz from it."

"What if you mess it up?" he teased, his eyes sparkling with humor.

"I never mess my ink up." I laughed at the thought. "Do you have any ink?"

He cocked an eyebrow at me, challengingly. "You tell me," he taunted. "Do you think I have ink?"

I loved that he was becoming confident enough around me that he was teasing me back.

I shook my head. No fucking way did he have ink

on him. I could be wrong but if he didn't, I wanted to get him in my chair when the time came that he did want ink.

"Nope. You are definitely an ink virgin, Sammy."

A glazed look passed his face when I said it. I wanted to kick myself. Of all the fucking words I could have used.

"In more ways than one," he replied, breaking our stare.

"You've been with girls before though..."

"Yeah. Several. It's just..." He sighed a deep breath before continuing. "I'm not ready to be with a man in that way."

I nodded my head. "To be honest, Sammy, I don't think I'm ready for that, either."

"Really?" His eyes widened in surprise at my words.

"Yeah. I'm not..." My hand tightened on my bottle. "One night stands have never been my scene." I carried on talking, feeling his stare on me. "To do that, you have to have complete trust. It's intimate and that's not something I would just do with anyone."

"So, you have done it before?" he asked.

"I have." I nodded my head, hoping that what I was about to tell him wouldn't turn him away from me. "I was in a relationship with someone. I thought he cared about me. Only he didn't."

Sammy's face fell at my words.

"From that day, I made sure that if I ever got involved with anyone again, that it would be based on more than just lies."

"So, you haven't been with anyone since him?" he asked.

"There have been girls. I'm not completely into boys but..." I shrugged. "Yeah, there have been a few girls."

He looked away, staring at the wall in front of us.

"But no one that really mattered. Not until you."

"Me?" He slowly turned his head back to me, nibbling on his bottom lip. "I matter?" He sounded so innocently naïve asking that question. "I don't think I've mattered in that way to someone before."

Before I could say anything, he quickly continued.

"I've never been in a serious relationship. There have been girls but no one that mattered," he confessed.

His words killed me. I wanted to matter to him. I wanted to be the one that he took a chance on. No. Not wanted: needed. I needed him to want to take a chance on me and that scared me. It scared me because I'd never wanted anyone in the way that I wanted him.

I held my hand out across the space between us and rested it on the cushion in between us, holding it palm up to him. The last time I did this, he'd pulled away, too afraid to touch me. I didn't want that again. I never wanted him to be afraid of me.

His eyes moved down to my hand where he stared at it for several moments. I could see the wheels turning in his head. He was thinking. Hopefully thinking of what I was offering. Thinking of my words about my past. I just hoped he was thinking about the right things.

Just as I went to pull my hand away defeated, he moved his hand closer before resting it on mine. Our finger slowly separated until they were entwined. We both let out a sigh of relief at the contact. Relief for me that he'd took that step and relief for him, most likely, due to how big that first step was.

"That wasn't so bad," he whispered, turning his gaze to me.

We were still sitting quite far apart but it was enough. His hand was in mine and I planned to keep it there. No matter what it took.

That's how we sat for a while. No words. Just his hand in mine.

It was complete bliss.

I slowly drained the last from my bottle. Slowly

because I didn't really want to part our hands but another was needed if I planned to keep him here longer.

"Do you want another one?" I asked, breaking the silence.

"Yeah, okay." His bottle was still half full but his admission obviously meant that he wanted to stay longer as well.

I grabbed two bottles from the fridge and popped the caps off. I turned around, ready to go back to spend a few more quiet moments with Sammy but froze in surprise. Sammy was standing right behind me, leaning against the middle unit in the kitchen.

"You frightened me." I chuckled, trying to relieve some of the tension. "Is everything okay?"

He nodded before straightening his shoulders back, rubbing his hand against his thigh. What he said next shocked me.

"Kiss me," he whispered.

Of all the things I imagined him saying to me, that was not it.

"What?" I choked, completely dumbstruck. "What did you say?"

I needed to hear him say it again. If that was what he wanted, he needed to vocalize it again. I couldn't fuck this up with him. Not with Sammy.

"I said, kiss me." He licked his bottom lip, before taking a step closer to me. "I want you to kiss me."

I hesitated briefly before reaching up and cupping his cheek. I rubbed my thumb across his cheekbone, hesitating. His skin was so soft. I could have stood there tracing my fingers over it for hours.

His eyes flickered down to my lips before darting back up to my eyes.

I slid my hand up and stroked the side of his hair, feeling the soft strands against my fingers.

He closed his eyes, a look of contentment on his face.

I moved my face closer to him, pressing my lips softly against his. His lips molded to mine, as he sucked gently on my bottom lip. Tremors moved down my spine when Sammy slid his arm around my waist, pulling me closer to him. I slid my other arm up, taking his face in my hands.

His chest pressed against mine. He groaned at the contact, moving backward so that he was leaning more against the worktop and pulling me with him. His hands slid up over my shoulders, threading his fingers into the back of my hair.

I groaned at the contact, loving the feel of him in my arms.

I pulled back, pressing my lips to his gently one last

time, before pulling away completely.

Staring at his lips, I just wanted to do it all over again. preferably somewhere more comfortable.

I trailed my hand down his arm and took his hand in mine. "Do you want to go back into the lounge?"

He frowned before gently squeezing my hand in his before his eyes moved past me. I felt like I was losing him to his inner thoughts and I was scared, trying to imagine what he could be thinking,

Suddenly, his face fell and I knew our night had come to an end.

"I have to go." He frowned. "I have training early in the morning and classes."

"That's okay." I nodded, accepting his answer. "Will I see you tomorrow?"

He turned away from me, leading me to the door before he turned around to face me.

"I'm sorry... I can't." He shook his head. "I shouldn't be here."

I frowned at the tone of his voice. He sounded frustrated.

Before I could say another word, he was out the door, running down the steps.

I walked back inside, slamming my door a little too forcefully.

I fucking knew it. Too soon.

FIVE
Sammy

Walking to the cafeteria the following day, I groaned when Logan looked at me. He had been giving me glances all morning and it was starting to do my head in.

"What?" I snapped. "What's the problem?"

His eyes narrowed briefly before he shook his head. "Nothing." He jogged ahead, grabbing the door and holding it open for me.

I cringed at my reply. If I couldn't handle Logan staring at me, how was I going to manage when the entire school would be staring at me when the time came.

I grabbed a sandwich and apple from the deli and joined Tillie and Johnny at their table while Logan crashed at a table of cheerleaders. I shook my head, chuckling. That boy would never settle down.

As I sat down, I noticed the way Johnny was holding Tillie to his side, like he couldn't bear to part from her. She turned her head and pressed a small kiss to his mouth, smiling sweetly as she pulled away.

Looking at them across the table, my mind immediately flashed back to the previous night.

I don't know what had come over me. It started with having my hand in his. It had felt good. No. It felt more than good. I'd wanted to know and feel what it was like. To be held by him. To be kissed by him.

It was perfect.

Perfect until I ran.

I shook my head, dismissing the memory and coming back to reality.

"Sammy," Tillie said, forcing my attention to her. "We didn't hear you come in last night."

"It was later than I planned." I shrugged my shoulders.

"Did you have a good time?" she asked, staring into my eyes.

She had the sweetest smile on her face and absolutely no judgment. Only concern and acceptance.

"I did." I nodded my head, trying hard not to think back on last night right then.

"So, when do we meet this special person?" Johnny asked, interrupting our conversation.

Special? Fuck, did Tillie tell him?

She mutely shook her head, not enough for anyone else to notice.

"Tillie told me that you may have met someone." He cocked an eyebrow at me, waiting. "So? When do we meet her?"

I breathed a sigh of relief at his words.

"Yeah," Logan chimed in, taking a seat beside me. "When do we meet this little hottie of yours?" He turned his cheeky grin to me.

"Not yet." I shook my head forcefully. "It's still new and the last thing I need is my crazy ass family scaring her away."

I was being crazy enough as it was.

I hated lying to people. It wasn't me. I was an honest person, and I didn't see the point in lies. Right then, though, it was necessary. At least, for the time being.

"Leave him alone," Tillie defended. "We'll meet this person when Sammy is ready for us to. Right?"

I smiled, nodding at her.

The conversation quickly changed direction and before we knew it, Logan was turning the direction to his medic credits.

"So, the coach has allowed me to withdraw from the team."

Johnny's face fell at his admission. Logan loved football but playing the actual sport bored the crap out of him. He was good at it but that was only due to his fitness regime. His passion would always be on the fitness and rehabilitation side of the sport.

"So, what's the plan now?" I asked, eager to hear more.

"I'll still have to be at every game but I'll be shadowing the medics. If I pass this year's modules, the coach said he'd be happy to offer me an internship with the team so that I can learn more hands-on skills."

"That's excellent!" Tillie announced, taking his hand in hers. "I'm so happy for you!"

"Thanks, Till." He grinned back at her, squeezing her hand gently in his.

"So, are we celebrating tonight or what?" Johnny asked.

"Not tonight," Logan said. "I have a date." He waggled his eyebrows and nodded his head towards the cheerleader table.

I turned my head and noticed there were several cheerleaders staring at Logan.

"Which one?" I asked, curious. None of them looked his type in all honesty.

"A gentleman never chooses." He sent a cheeky wink in Tillie's direction before leaving us and walking out of the cafeteria.

"So, are we seeing you tonight?" Tillie asked. "We could catch up with a Disney movie!"

I laughed loudly at her suggestion. Tillie loved Disney movies. We all had to suffer for it when she was in one of her Disney moods. Luckily, Logan and I could often escape it but Johnny couldn't.

"As tempting as that sounds, I think I'll pass."

Her face fell for a second before she turned to look at Johnny. "You won't desert me, will you?" She smiled up at him with a teasing glint in her eye.

"Never, sweetheart."

I rolled my eyes at how cheesy they were. They were enough to make you sick.

"See you later, lovebirds."

I gave them a small wave and began walking home. My thoughts slowly drifted to Benjamin and I began wondering what he was doing. Was he having a good day? Was he continuously thinking about last night like I was?

Walking inside, I stole a quick cookie from the jar before going upstairs and changing into my gym pants and a black t-shirt. Grabbing my keys, I locked up and began my run. I had been slacking lately, but it was good to get my feet back to pounding the sidewalk.

Before I knew it, my feet had taken me back to the college grounds and I was making a few laps around the field before jogging back home.

When I had started college, the field where we trained and played our games became a place where I felt most at peace. After the incident with Lucy, though, the field was where I felt the most stressed. Looking around, I saw that part of my life was slowly dying. I could be as carefree as I wanted but my arm wasn't responding.

I knew that. I didn't need some man in a white coat to tell me that.

"Hey, kid." I looked up and saw the coach walking towards me. "How are we doing?" He took a seat next to me, seeming concerned.

"Nothing much." I shook my head. "Just thinking."

"About the game?" He cocked an eyebrow, looking at me patiently.

"That and other stuff." I looked back across the field. "My arm isn't as strong as I would like it to be."

"I know." He sighed, sounding frustrated before he shook his head dismissively. "I wouldn't panic yet, kid. We still have a few weeks." He clapped me on the back before he stood, leaving me to my thoughts.

Was I panicking too early? Was I putting too much stress on my arm and letting it affect my thoughts when it came to Benjamin? Was I being unfair to Benjamin?

Yes. I was being unfair. Benjamin had demonstrated to me that he only wanted to know me and possibly have more with me but... I didn't think I was ready. There was so much pressure. If I came out and publicised my relationship with Benjamin, what would that say about me? What would it say about Johnny? Or Logan?

I didn't want anyone else to suffer for my choices. Johnny was so loved and admired in this town and I didn't want this to affect whatever career choices may come his way.

I was scared.

I also didn't want Benjamin to suffer, though. Maybe he would be better off with someone that didn't have all this baggage.

I shook my head, making my way back home. As I entered my block, I saw Bex standing on my doorstep, waving at me awkwardly. As I got closer, she straightened up her posture, giving me her full attention.

"Hey, Sammy." She walked towards me and pulled

me into a hug, squeezing me extra tight before letting me go.

"What are you doing here?" I asked, rubbing my palm across her upper back.

"I thought you might need someone to talk to." She pulled back, rubbing her hand up and down the top of my arm.

"Sure. Come on in." I jogged up the stairs with Bex following me.

Walking into my room, I shut the door after us and sat down on the bed.

"So, what do you want to talk about?" I asked nonchalantly.

"Sammy..." She had a gentleness to her tone. She sat next to me, taking my hand in hers and resting it on her lap. "You can talk to me."

I shrugged my shoulders, looking at the door. "What should I say?"

"That you're struggling?" She rubbed her thumb soothingly across the back of my hand. "It's natural— natural to be scared."

"I'm not scared!" I defended, hating that she was spot on with her words. "It's just..."

What could I possibly say? I couldn't bullshit Bex. Not when she'd already been through all the confusion I was currently feeling.

"Sammy, it's hard telling the family. There's so much pressure." She sighed before turning to look at me. "But you are so much luckier than the rest of us."

I turned to her, confused by her words.

"You have the most supportive family. They are not going to react negatively." She smiled at me warmly. "I promise you."

"I keep thinking that maybe I'm wrong. That maybe, I'm just reading into my feelings for Benjamin wrongly?" I ended it as a question.

"Feelings?" She cocked an eyebrow before a wicked grin covered her face. "I didn't know we were at feelings stage."

I rolled my eyes at her taunting. That didn't take long.

"Maybe there aren't any feelings. Maybe I'm just confused with everything happening and I'm..."

I was grasping for straws at this point and I wasn't fooling anyone. Least of all her.

"Have you guys kissed?" She cocked an inquisitive eyebrow.

I nodded, looking away.

"Is that where the feelings came?" she asked, lowering her head to look in my eyes. "Did it feel...?" She left her question open, waiting for me to fill in the blanks.

I shrugged my shoulders. I didn't know how to answer that question. This conversation had slowly moved into an uncomfortable territory.

"Look, I just..."

"Kiss me," she demanded, interrupting.

I chuckled. "What?" I asked, wondering where the hell her words came from. Why would she want me to kiss her?

I stood up, trying to get some space between us. "Look, Bex..." I said, turning to address her. Before I could say anything else, she rolled her eyes, taking my chin in between her thumb and forefinger.

"You heard me." She looked up at me. "I want you to kiss me."

She slowly slid her hand up around my neck and threaded her fingers through the back of my hair. She leaned up on her tiptoes and pressed her lips softly to mine.

I closed my eyes, sucking on her soft bottom lip. I slipped my arm around her waist and pulled her to me, molding our bodies closer to each other. Her other hand slid up until it was pressed against my heart. After a few moments, she pulled away, giving me a small smile.

"Now answer me one question," she whispered. "Did that feel better than when you kissed him?"

I could lie. I wanted to lie. I wanted to scream and cry. I wanted to throw her on the bed and hold her to me and tell her that she was the one that made me feel alive. But I didn't.

I shook my head negatively and her eyes filled with sympathy.

"Come here, sweetheart." She held her arms open to me, offering me comfort.

I went willingly, letting her hold me and rock me from side to side. I could feel my chest tighten at the comfort she was giving me and for the first time, I let it go. I let all the emotions, frustration, anger, confusion, resentment and fear leave my body. It came out as a quiet sob, my tears leaving a wet trail down her neck and soaking into her vest.

"I've got you, Sammy." She slid her hand up to cup the back of my head. "It's okay. It's going to be okay." Her voice was tense and I knew she was holding back her own emotions.

I crushed her to me tighter, never wanting to let go.

An hour later, we were both lying on my bed, just our hands touching.

"So, what do I do now?" I asked, voicing my thoughts.

She turned her head to face me before answering. "Whatever you want to happen."

"I'm not ready to tell the boys," I admitted.

"Then don't tell them." She sighed before turning on her side to face me. "Only tell people when you're ready to tell them. Don't ever let someone force you into doing something you don't want to do." She tucked her hands beneath her cheek, resting them on the pillow. "Get comfortable with it first before telling your family. Make sure that this guy is worth it."

"What do you mean?" I was confused by her words.

"Get to know him. See where this thing goes."

"I ran away from him last night," I admitted, tucking my arm beneath my head to prop myself up a little.

"That's my point, Sammy. You have to be comfortable in yourself and in any relationship you choose to have with him before you can even expect to tell people."

I nodded at her words. That made sense.

"And remember," she said seriously. "If you choose to admit to those around you that you're gay, do it for you. Not for anyone else." She pressed her lips together thinking before she continued. "If Benjamin is as crazy about you as he should be, he'll wait. He'll be patient. You're worth the wait."

I turned to her, smiling for the first time. I silently lifted my arm and she scooted over, resting her head on my chest. I leaned down and pressed a small kiss on her forehead before resting my head on top of hers.

"Thank you, Bex."

"You're welcome, Sammy." She cuddled into my chest, squeezing me. "So, how are you going to get back into this guy's good books?"

I thought for a few minutes, needing to do something. I pulled my phone out of my pocket and googled 'Wicked Ink'. I pressed dial and waited for Lily to pick up.

"Wicked Ink. How can I help?" her cheery voice echoed down the line.

"Lily, it's Sammy. I need your help with something."

"Of course, sugar. What can I do?"

SIX

Benjamin

Walking home from Wicked Ink, I was ready to kick my shoes off and chill. The boys were going out for a few beers but I'd had to pass. I wasn't in the mood to socialize or pick up some random guy like they suggested to get Sammy out of my system.

But I wanted him in my system. I wasn't ready to move on or give up on that yet. I wasn't ready to walk away. He needed time. How much I wasn't sure, but I wasn't that much of an asshole to just give up on someone when they had no clue which way was left or right. I'd be here for as long as he needed me to be.

When I thought back to how we'd left things, I got

frustrated. I'd pushed and pushed and I shouldn't have.

I slid the key into the lock and kicked my shoes off, heading straight for the bathroom. A shower was needed. I'd pulled an all-dayer to cover Tyler's morning shift and I was ready to just kick back and relax.

After taking a too long shower that had me freezing my balls off as I got out, I wrapped a fluffy towel around my waist and made my way to the bedroom. I quickly changed into my gym pants and white t-shirt and made my way to the kitchen. Looking through the cupboards, my stomach gurgled, demanding food, but I just couldn't be bothered. After the week I'd had, I just wanted to shut everything out and disappear for a few days. My food hunt was disturbed when there was a knock on the door.

I groaned, making my way to it. I really wasn't in the mood for visitors.

I looked through the peephole, checking who it was. I was always worried that my old man would one day track me down and give me another battering. I knew I was older now, and stockier, but he was still family. I didn't think I could ever physically hurt him in the way he hurt me. Family or not.

I froze, surprised when I saw who was on the other

side of my door. I grabbed the door handle and quickly turned it, pulling the door open.

"Sammy, what are you doing here?" I was not expecting him to appear on my doorstep so soon after last night.

"Can I come in?" His eyes flicked down to my chest and straight back to my eyes.

I nodded, holding the door open wider for him. He had his backpack with him, making me wonder what the hell he had inside it.

"I want to say I'm sorry for last night. It was unfair and I should never have done it."

I was shaking my head before he had even finished. "You never have to apologize for that. I pushed and it was too much, I guess."

"You didn't push." He lifted his foot and tapped the toe against the floor. "I panicked. I started freaking out and I..." He shrugged. "I just bolted."

"You're allowed to freak out, Sammy." He was so busy staring at the floor avoiding my gaze and I hated it. I walked closer to him until we were toe to toe. I took his face in my hands and slowly tilted his face up to me. His deep green eyes met mine. "Just don't run from me, okay? Stay and talk to me."

He nodded his assent, his eyes briefly darting down to my lips.

Did he want me to kiss him? I wanted to kiss him but I was afraid it would just be a repeat of last night. I was afraid that the last thing I'd see again would be him running out my door, away from me.

"Can I kiss you?" I asked, voicing my thoughts.

He nodded, his lips parting slightly.

"You won't run?" I asked, half teasing.

He slid his hands up and placed them on mine still holding his face. "I won't run," he whispered.

I dipped my head down slowly, gazing into his eyes. We both had the same shade of green in our eyes and I loved staring into them. He closed his eyes just before our lips met, giving himself over. I could feel it in the way he hummed against my lips as I applied the gentlest of pressure.

His hands slid down from where I was holding him and he gently pressed them against my sides, fisting my t-shirt in his hands. I pulled back after pressing several soft kisses to his lips, needing to see his eyes.

Please don't run.

I couldn't handle it if he ran again.

He smiled up at me, looking sexy as fuck.

I breathed a sigh of relief, causing Sammy to chuckle. His hand slid up to his back strap, fidgeting with it.

"What's in the bag?" I asked, curious.

He grinned, lowering the bag from his shoulders. "Only the best movie trilogy ever created."

He looked so excited. It made me want to kiss him again.

I tossed my head back laughing when I saw what he pulled out of his bag.

"The original Star Wars trilogy?"

I didn't think he could get any more perfect if he tried. Cute and sexy, hot football player and he had an inner nerd.

"I don't suppose you brought food as well?"

He grinned at me, pulling a scrunched up Chinese leaflet out of his back pocket. "Only the best in town."

Several hours later, we were in the middle of 'The Empire Strikes Back'—which is by far the best film of the series. We were both stuffed after the best Chinese food; Sammy was definitely right about that.

He was currently slumped down on the couch, grinning at the TV. He'd get this cutest smile on his face whenever R2-D2 appeared on the screen. It was super cute and very nerdy but I didn't say anything. It was one of his little quirks and I was loving learning these little things about him.

Before I could look away, he turned his head and caught me staring.

"So, who is your favorite character?" he asked.

I looked away, pretending to mull it over. "I would have to go with Obi-Wan. Yours?"

"I'm sure you already know." He grinned at me, looking bashful.

"I'd have to go with R2."

He nodded making me question it.

"Why? What is it about R2 that you love so much?"

He shrugged, looking back to the screen before back to me. "I don't know. He's bad ass, always gets Luke out of trouble. Plus, he started this entire story with Leia and the plans hidden in him."

I grinned at the way he rambled. It was very cute.

I looked down at his hand resting on the sofa in between us and before I knew what I was doing, I had moved my hand and stroked my finger over his wrist. I looked up at him, waiting for some anxiety or stress to appear in his expression.

It never did.

He closed his eyes, a faint smile appearing on his face. "That feels nice," he whispered.

I sighed, feeling relief course through me. He didn't pull away. He liked my touch.

I focused back on the screen, continuing my stroking pattern on his wrist through the rest of the film. Before I knew it, the credits were rolling. I looked over and saw that Sammy's head was resting on the back of the sofa. It looked like I had relaxed him too much.

I chuckled, turning the TV off and relaxing back into my position. Looking over, I smiled when I saw the sexiest pout on his face. It was very kissable. Before I knew it, his body tensed and he shot up, grabbing onto the cushion. All color drained from his face and his chest was heaving.

He looked terrified.

"Sammy? Are you...?"

He shot up out of his seat. Fuck, what happened? Was he going to run?

"Sammy, wait..." I ran after him, clasping my hand down on his shoulder.

He spun around, looking angry and scared. Very scared. He threw his arms around me, pushing his face into my neck. His body shook and he tightened his arms around me.

"Hey," I soothed him, rubbing my hand up and down his back. "It's okay."

I frowned when I felt wetness soak into my top. Fuck, did this happen often?

I held him to me tighter and slowly rocked us from side to side. I pressed a kiss to his hairline, wanting to offer as much comfort as I could. I hated seeing him in pain. I wanted to take it all. Take away every sob, every scar, every tear.

After a while, he pulled away. His cheeks were colored red and he avoided looking at me.

I took his hand in mine and pulled him back to the sofa. "Come and sit."

He followed me, taking his seat. He stared at the coffee table, ignoring my gaze.

I rubbed his knee soothingly. "Talk to me."

"It's nothing." He shook his head. "Forget it. It's stupid."

"Nothing that bothers you is stupid."

He was silent for a few minutes before he started talking.

"At the start of this college year, she moved across the street from us. Her name is Tillie."

He looked at me before he grabbed my hand and pulled it into his lap. Shivers shot up my arm from the contact. I loved it when he touched me.

"I live with my older brother Johnny and they are together now." He bit his lip briefly before continuing. "One thing led to another and one day, Tillie went to my house after classes. Only Johnny's psychotic ex-fuck buddy was in the house. She attacked Johnny and waited there for Tillie."

Fucking hell. I wrapped my fingers around his hand, squeezing gently. No wonder he had fucking nightmares.

"I'd been training late and had my bike with me. I usually keep it in the back so I went through the back door. Just as I went to open the door, my phone vibrated with a text message from Logan." His eyes flicked to mine.

"What did it say?" I asked.

"Do not go in the house." He shrugged. "I didn't listen. I knew it must have been bad for Logan to warn me but I didn't listen. You don't listen when it comes to family. Right?" It broke me how unsure he sounded.

I nodded my head vigorously, needing him to continue—needing to know how the story ended.

"She had a gun pointed at Johnny. I crept close enough that Lucy didn't see me, but I was going to be late." He took a deep breath. "I reacted. I shot forward and pushed Johnny out of the way."

"Where was Tillie?" The words flew out of my

mouth. I knew that Tillie was okay. I had seen her with Sammy many times since then but...

"She was behind Johnny." His eyes came up to mine and stayed on me. "I'm bigger than her and I thought I could take the bullet. It didn't work and we were both hurt by it." His eyes filled with tears and it killed me. "That's what my dreams are about. They are about not getting there in time or getting there too late. Sometimes it's Johnny on the floor covered in blood. Sometimes it's Tillie."

I lifted my hand from his and trailed it up and rested it on his chest. I had no words. I was floored by his courage and what he was willing to do for Tillie.

"You're a hero," I whispered, unable to keep the awe from my voice. "You saved her."

He shrugged his shoulders dismissively, not accepting my words.

"It's what you do for family."

He was right. I'd do anything for Lily and she'd do anything for me. Tillie was probably no different when it came to Sammy.

"You're pretty special, aren't you?" I said it more to myself but I also wanted him to know how amazing he was. We all say that we would do anything for our families but it takes a lot to actually step up and risk our life for another. "Look at me." I turned his face to me, needing to see those green eyes of his.

I stared into them, wanting him to know that I was serious. He was very special.

"I really want to kiss you," I whispered. I rubbed my thumb along his cheekbone, loving the feel of his soft skin.

"I want you to kiss me," he whispered. His pink tongue peeked out and licked his bottom lip.

I shifted closer and he did the same. I dipped my head down and pressed my lips to his. Kissing Sammy was slowly becoming my addiction. His taste was unlike any other and I didn't think I could ever get sick of it.

I was trying to be patient and gentle with Sammy, especially with all the stress he has been under with this decision, but now that I had my lips on his, I was finding it hard to remain a gentleman. I just wanted to press him down and feel him under me.

He slid his hand up my arm before threading it into the back of my hair. I groaned, pressing my lips firmer against his. Hands in my hair were my 'on' button and Sammy had learned that a little too fast.

I arched my body closer to his, needing to feel him against me.

He pressed his other hand against my chest, gripping my t-shirt in his fist. He tensed, stopping me from pushing him down.

I immediately tensed and began to pull away. "Too much?" I asked, worried.

He shook his head. "You look kind of uncomfortable."

I sighed, frustrated. "I'm trying to be patient. And gentle. And I don't want to freak you out."

He laughed, rolling his eyes at me. "I have kissed girls before."

"I know." I felt like an idiot for bringing this up. "But this is different and I... I don't want to fuck this up."

"You won't," he whispered. "Would this be easier?"

He turned towards me, placing his hands on top of my shoulders and shuffled closer. He slid his leg over my body, resting his weight above mine.

Would this be easier? Fuck, yes. Would it be more difficult to keep myself in check in this position? Abso-fucking-lutely.

I tensed, swallowing harshly before nodding. I tilted my head upwards, wanting his lips back on mine. I waited patiently, letting him stay in control.

He slowly lowered his face, pressing his lips to mine. He shakily exhaled against me.

I leaned my head backward, pressing it into the cushion. My hands touched against his sides, needing something to hold.

He gasped at my touch, his lips parting. His tongue softly moved against mine and I was done for. I was his. In whatever capacity he wanted me.

I parted my lips more and allowed his tongue entry. It entwined with mine and the only thought I had was why hadn't we been doing this sooner. I groaned, my hands tightening on his shirt, pulling him against me.

His lips were molded to mine, making it impossible for me to concentrate. He moved his mouth from mine and trailed his lips down my neck, pressing soft and gentle kisses as he went. His tongue peeked out and licked against the juncture of my shoulder.

I gasped, my hips automatically shifting and rocking against his. I groaned in frustration. Damn traitorous body.

He pulled back, shifting his body away slightly. "I'm not ready for that," he whispered.

I closed my eyes in frustration. "I know. I can go slow."

"You'd do that for me?" he asked, that shy little smile of his peeking out again.

"For you, I will."

SEVEN

Sammy

"For you, I will."

He was a good man. I knew that. I wanted to believe that.

Benjamin had been so patient with me. Every time that I'd run or got nervous, he'd remained his calm and gentle self. He could have made things difficult for me when I ran but he didn't. He was still his kind, caring and understanding self.

My attention was taken when my phone began vibrating on the coffee table. I pulled back, standing to grab it. I cringed when I saw I had three missed calls from Tillie. My fingers flew over the keypad, telling her I was on my way home.

It was almost midnight. She was probably freaking out.

"I have to go," I said, turning to him.

His face fell in what I assumed was disappointment.

It made me smile. I was happy that he didn't want me to go. The feeling was mutual.

"Maybe we can watch the next movie tomorrow evening?" he asked hopefully.

"I'd like that," I said nodding. "I could come over after class?"

"Don't you have training tomorrow?" he asked, cocking an eyebrow at me.

"Not tomorrow." I shook my head. "I always jog in the morning so that'll be my training for the day."

"I get off work about 7 pm."

I smiled at him, loving the faint blush that covered his cheeks

"I'd like that." He walked towards me and took my hand in his, leading me to the door.

Shivers shot up my arm from his touch. Every time he touched me, he left a blaze of heat.

He pulled the door open and stood to the side. "I'll see you tomorrow, then."

I looked up at him, confused by my feelings. If I was out with a girl, this would normally be the part where I would kiss her. Was he waiting for me to kiss him? Did I want to kiss him?

Before I could get too lost, he leaned forward and gave me a quick kiss on the lips.

I smiled up at him. "Bye."

He winked at me as I went. Fuck, I was lost to him.

Walking home, I thought over the last few hours, smiling to myself when I realized that tonight had gone well. Better than I expected it to go. Being with another man, I expected there to be some level of awkwardness but there hadn't been. When I told him about the shooting, I found only acceptance.

I cringed when I saw that the lights were still on. It was something I had slowly become used to. Many times I would come home late and find Tillie waiting up for me. It wasn't the first time that Tillie had stayed up waiting for me. Since the shooting, she and I had become very protective of each other. She may have been tiny, but she could be a little hurricane if you pissed her off.

I toed my shoes off at the door and grinned when I saw her and Johnny camped out on the sofa. Johnny was sleeping but Tillie was cuddled up next to him, reading a book. I leaned my shoulder against the wall watching them. Her eyes slowly tilted up to mine before she marked her place with a bookmark.

"You didn't have to wait up for me," I softly admonished her.

"We didn't." She shook her head, wrapping her blanket tighter around her.

The movement caused Johnny to stir and his head slowly turned in my direction. "You're home."

Tillie was a terrible liar. I chuckled, taking a few steps back. "I'm going to bed."

Jogging up the stairs, I quickly changed into my shorts and crashed.

When I woke up the next day, I felt good. Better even.

I spent most of my day in between classes stuck in the library. The time was supposed to be spent on research, but my mind was stuck in a constant loop. My appointment with the team's doctors was fast approaching. I thought I would be nervous. Or scared.

I felt neither.

I knew what the doctors were going to say. My arm wasn't responding to the strength conditioning the way that it should. It was nowhere near as strong as it should be expected to be to catch a ball at high speeds. My days on this team were numbered.

I was prepared for it. Johnny remained hopeful,

but I knew my body better than anyone else. I didn't need a doctor to evaluate me and tell me what I knew was true.

Leaving the library and heading home, I groaned at how early it was. Benjamin didn't finish for another two hours. I saw Joy up ahead, sitting on her deck. She was knitting and her attention looked a million miles away.

I ran into the house, dumped my bag and ran upstairs to do a quick change of clothes. I slipped my blue t-shirt on with my blue jeans and sneakers and left.

Walking over to Joy's, I smiled at her.

She smiled without even lifting her head, knowing that I was there. "Fancy a cup of tea?"

"I would love a cup of tea," I responded, opening her gate and stepping through.

I followed her inside, taking a seat at her kitchen table while she pottered around. I would have offered to help but she'd only have waved me off. A few minutes later, she was joining me at the table, placing a piece of coconut cake in front of me.

I know footballers are supposed to stay in shape, but Joy's coconut cake was to die for. No way was I going to turn that down. I fed a small bit into my mouth, moaning at the taste.

She chuckled before she began talking. "So how is school going?"

"It's good." I nodded my head. "I spend most of today at the library."

"And how are things with everyone else?" She had a warm smile on her face but there was also a bit of concern in her eyes.

I sighed, frustrated with myself. I was a complete idiot. Ever since I had spoken to Joy about Benjamin, I hadn't seen her much. She had probably been worrying about me.

"It's been... stressful." I chuckled. That was the only word I could use. "But also amazing at the same time?"

She nodded her head, indicating for me to continue.

"Benjamin and I have established a relationship of sorts."

Was it a relationship? Could I call it that? I mean, I know I wasn't interested in anyone else. Was he? I assumed it was only me he was spending his time with, but I guess I really didn't know.

"I talked to Bex about it."

"Good choice." She nodded her head, tapping the top of my hand soothingly. "She would know how to help."

I nodded, agreeing with her. "She said that I shouldn't be stressing about telling people. That I should focus on getting comfortable first and get to know Benjamin more. To see if he's worth the risk that I would be taking."

"Sound advice. So, things with him are going well?" she asked, curiously.

"At the moment. I'm seeing him later tonight."

"Well, he sounds like a nice man. I look forward to meeting him one day."

I smiled, bringing her hand to my lips and pressing a kiss to her knuckles. "He'll love you."

I spent the next few minutes demolishing the rest of my cake and tea.

Leaving Joy's, I began walking in the direction of the coffee shop near Wicked Ink. The same coffee shop where Benjamin had walked up to me and made me have a major freak out.

Walking in, my eyes went straight to the menu board above the counter. I wasn't a fan of all the creamy coffee choices they offered here. I liked my coffee black. No fussing.

I spun around surprised when I felt a hand tap against my jean-clad ass pocket. Lily beamed at me with a cheeky smile on her face.

"Shouldn't you be a few shops up?" She pointed

her head sideways indicating the direction of Wicked Ink.

I laughed, loving the way that she put things. She was straight and to the point. She was basically a female version of Logan. "I was just getting a coffee."

"By yourself?" She looked around the café before looking back at me.

I nodded, confused. Who else would I be with?

"Oh, great." A relieved expression covered her face. "You can help me carry the drinks back."

"How many drinks do you have to carry?" I cocked a pointed eyebrow at her, knowing full well what she was up to.

"I'm small and dainty," she defended with an innocent expression on her face.

She was far from innocent. More like innocently wicked.

"Plus, I have sugary treats to carry. You wouldn't want me to fall and hurt myself."

I rolled my eyes at her Oscar-worthy performance and quickly ordered my coffee. I had no plans on seeing Benjamin until later that night, so now he'd probably think I was stalking him or something.

As I waited for the barista to serve my coffee, Lily spoke up from behind me.

"He's been smiling like a goofball all day." I turned

to look down at her and was surprised by the depth of emotion I saw reflected in her eyes. "Happy looks good on him."

That made me smile. I knew I wasn't the easiest guy to be around with our situation but the fact that he was smiling said it all.

"Of course, he's staring at the clock all day and doing my head in but..." She sighed dramatically, rolling her eyes. "I suppose I can put up with it."

I let her squeeze past me so that she could put her order in. Listening to her sound her order off to the barista, I chuckled to myself. She really was going to need a hand in carrying this stuff.

She turned towards me, laughing at the look on my face. "All the boys are in today," she explained. "They had a full back piece and could only fit him into the books in a certain amount of time. So, the poor guy has had three tattooists working on him."

"Ouch!" I replied, not liking the sound of that. I had never really been into tattoos but that sounded painful.

She giggled, taking the boxes of sugary goods off the barista and handing them straight to me. She had enough to feed a small army.

"Some are for the house as well," she explained, reading my thoughts. "Trix has a sweet tooth."

I nodded and followed her from the shop, letting her lead the way.

She opened the door and held it with her hip so that I could pass without it slamming on me. We dumped them all on the counter and were soon descended upon by Tyler and Darren.

"Hands off." She tapped Tyler's knuckles. "That's my muffin."

He rumpled her hair, causing her to frown. "You even brought something that wasn't on the menu." Tyler and Darren both stared at me, smirking.

I chuckled, feeling anxiety creep up my spine.

"Leave him alone," Lily said. "He's right through there, Sammy." She pointed to Benjamin's room and I made my way in that direction, eager to escape.

I walked around the corner and smiled when I saw him at the sink again. I walked in, not wanting to disturb him and took a seat in the tattoo chair. I lifted my feet and made myself at home. I closed my eyes, surprisingly comfortable in the chair that was known to inflict so much pain when the gun was in operation.

After a while, the sound of Benjamin's movements stopped and the room went silent.

I opened my eyes, a smile appearing on my face. He was leaning his weight back against the worktop, drying his hands with a towel.

"You look very comfortable there." He chuckled, gathering up the small pots and putting them on the worktop.

"I could fall asleep in this chair," I replied. I was feeling very sleepy sitting there.

He tossed his head back, laughing. "That's the first time I've heard that."

"I hope it's okay that I came by." I was starting to worry what he was thinking. The few times that I had see benjamin, I could normally read him. He tended to be very open, but right now, he was unreadable. It was like a mask had slipped into place. "Lily needed help carrying the cakes and..." I was stammering.

He walked forward and placed his finger over my lips.

"It's more than okay. I'm happy to see you." He grinned, holding his hand out for me.

I took it and stood, groaning at the pain in my shoulder.

"You okay?" he frowned, looking between my eyes and my shoulder. "Is it from the bullet?"

I groaned, flexing my arm. "Yeah. It's not as strong as it used to be and I'm still in therapy with it."

He nodded, lifting himself on to the worktop behind him.

I looked at him, trying to determine where the rest

of his tattoos were. I wasn't used to seeing tattooists with such little ink showing. I stupidly assumed that tattooists were covered head to toe in ink. However, these guys weren't. Tyler had little bits of ink peeking out from beneath his t-shirt on his arms and neck and Lily had tattoos behind her ears but I couldn't see any on Benjamin besides the little square of blue ink that would peek out beneath the sleeve of his t-shirt.

"Can you please not look at me like that?" he asked. His voice sounded strained.

"Why?" I whispered. Why didn't he want me looking at him?

"Because you're making me want to do things that you and I are both not ready for."

Lust shot through me at the fire that reflected back at me in the pools of his eyes.

I bit down on my bottom lip, wanting to know what he was thinking. It was true that I wasn't ready for sex; that was too much of a step and it would be too fast. I needed time when it came to that, but I couldn't deny that I was attracted to him. His mind and body.

"Come here," Benjamin whispered.

I stepped forward, secretly loving the way that his eyes trailed up and down my body. They kept coming back to my chest and resting there for a fraction before moving up to my face. When I was close enough, his hands softly pressed against my ribs and pulled me forward.

I stepped in between his legs with a few inches of space separating us. We were close last night on his sofa but this oddly felt more intimate.

Last night he was a gentleman; right now, I was seeing a different side of him. Benjamin had been so sweet with me but I was seeing a rougher side to him.

I placed my hands on his arms, feeling the coarse hairs before trailing them up his upper arms. I loved the feel of his skin beneath mine. It was very different to a woman's warm skin. More rough and strong.

His hand trailed up my back before he threaded his long fingers into the back of my hair. He looked concerned, almost as if he was doubting his actions.

I hated to see doubt there. I was right where I wanted to be.

"Kiss me," I whispered, voicing what he and I both wanted.

He judged my reaction before his lips slowly descended on mine.

I gasped as sparks erupted from his touch and I closed my eyes, giving myself over to him. I stepped closer, wanting to be near him, feel him more with my touch.

"You guys are so cute!" Lily screeched from the door, making me jump back.

"You scared the crap out of me!" I chuckled, putting my hand on my chest dramatically.

She giggled before turning to Benjamin. "Your 6 pm is here."

Benjamin nodded. He looked at me and my eyes immediately went to his lips. I wanted to do that again, only this time with no interruptions.

"Sammy can come and sit with me if you like?"

I nodded, following her from the room with that kiss on constant repeat with every step I took away from him.

EIGHT

Benjamin

It was past 7 pm before I finished up the last of the tattoo.

It was our policy that all designs should be agreed upon when the appointment is made and the deposit is paid. Instead, I had a young lady that couldn't make up her mind between three different designs. She finally decided on having a rosary wrapped around her wrist with her children's initials dangling from them.

After taking a photo of her newly tatted wrist in a few angles to add to our portfolio, she was on her way to pay Lily. I groaned, rolling the muscles of my shoulders. Pulling an all-dayer fucking killed my back.

After cleaning up my workstation, I grabbed my keys and made my way to the front, where Sammy was hopefully still waiting. I chuckled when I saw him staring at a tribal piece on the wall.

"What does this mean?" He grinned, turning towards me. "Does it mean anything?"

He sounded so excited. Almost as though he was considering it.

"It means family," Lily chirped up from her spot at the counter. "It's never been tatted on anyone."

"Lily loves to have art pieces from college students put up on the wall. Says it may inspire fresh ideas from the clients and ourselves." I rolled my eyes jokingly. "It hasn't worked but we let her have her fun."

"Jerk," she muttered under her breath. She had a smirk on her face so I knew that she was kidding.

"You ready to go?" Sammy asked, turning to face us.

My eyes trailed down, wanting nothing more than to drag him back to my workstation and repeat earlier but with the way Lily was smirking at us, she knew exactly what I wanted to do.

"Yeah, let's go." I waved Lily to the door, insisting on being the one to lock up. She was too short to reach the rolling shutter anyway.

"See you later boys." She gave us both a kiss on the cheek before she was skipping down the street, her hair blowing in the breeze behind her. She looked like a demented fairy gone wrong.

We waited until she got to her apartment building and after a quick wave, she was in the door.

We started walking home to my place when I saw a couple walking towards us. The guy was twirling the girl before taking her hand in his and pulling her closer to his side.

Jealousy shot through me.

I wanted to do that. Not the twirling thing but the hand holding thing. I wanted to reach for Sammy's hand and have him let me take it. I didn't like hiding things but with Sammy, there was no other choice. He wasn't ready and I didn't want another rejection.

I looked over at him, loving the way his hair would flop over his forehead. Sammy was perfect without even trying. When we were together, we seemed to just fit seamlessly without any struggle. Without even trying.

As we approached my apartment building, I began fidgeting. I didn't mean to. I wasn't normally a fidgeter. I was usually calm and in control, but lately, that had gone out the window. If I was in a relationship with someone or whatever it was that Sammy and I had, it was usually a lot more hands on than my current situation.

Not that I was a sex freak or a player in the dating world but I tended to get passionate about the people in my life. This was the first time I had to keep a leash on that side of myself. I didn't want to rush anything with him but there were only so many times a guy could jack off in the shower.

Sammy was testing my patience in every way.

I slid the key in, thinking of ways to keep my hands to myself. Sammy was new to all of this, I had to keep reminding myself, and the last thing he needed was me acting like a horny fucker and trying to dry hump him.

I looked back at Sammy and saw a worried look on his face.

"What's wrong?" I asked, tossing my keys on the table. He hadn't looked like that when we left Wicked Ink.

"I, uh..." He cleared his throat. "You've been... you were kind of quiet on the way home."

Fucking idiot. Of course he would think the worst. I had gotten so lost in my thoughts that he was now thinking something was wrong.

"I was just thinking." I placed my hands on the back of my head, feeling stressed.

"Are you sure it's not...?" He didn't finish his question but I knew what he was thinking. He thought it was him.

"It's not you." I dropped my arms, trying to ease some of the tension in my body.

He looked away, avoiding my gaze. It pissed me off. Sammy never had to look away from me.

I growled in frustration and walked up to him, taking his face in my hands. I was being rough with him but I was horny and now pissed off that he thought he had done something.

"It's not you." I stared into his eyes and cocked an eyebrow at him. "Okay?"

I waited for the worry and frustration to ease from his eyes until only my Sammy remained.

My Sammy? Fuck, I was jumping the gun with this guy. We had only kissed a handful of times and I didn't even know what we were to each other and I was already calling him mine.

"Then what is it?" he asked. His breath was a sweet whisper across my face.

I wanted nothing more than to let it go. To be completely honest with him in the way that he was with me. I was a hypocrite. I was scared that if I completely honest with him, it would scare him and he'd pull away from me.

"I want you," I whispered, smoothing the hair away from his face. "This would normally be the stage where sex would be involved and I..." I sighed deeply, struggling to find the words. "I just want you."

I was expecting revulsion or some tension but it didn't come. Nothing came. He just continued to stare at me. His eyes were so deep that I wanted nothing more than to fall into them. Fall and never come back.

He sighed out a shaky breath before he spoke. "I'm not ready for that."

And here came the rejection.

"But I..." he continued. He took a shaky gulp. "But more would be nice."

"More?" I asked.

He had to lead me. I couldn't push too fast. I was scared that my actions would push him away. I couldn't let that happen. I wanted Sammy to want me as much as I wanted him. Sadly, patience and I didn't get along very well.

"More of you." He shrugged, almost as if he didn't know how to explain. "Just more of us."

"More of this?" I turned my head and kissed his cheek. "Or this?" Kiss to the other cheek. "Or this?" I pressed a kiss to his neck, loving the sexy tremor that moved through his body.

He nodded at my words. His breathing had deepened and his cheeks had a slight pink to them. It looked sexy as hell on him.

He moved his hands and placed them on my stomach before he slowly moved them up to my chest.

The feel of his hands on my body was not helping. Sammy usually only touched me on my sides or back. The feel of him touching my chest made me want to slam my body against his and show him just how much I desired him.

His hands moved across my chest where his palms gently moved over my nipples.

I was fucking gone.

I slammed my lips on his, causing him to gasp. I moved my tongue against his, groaning at the taste of him. I would never get enough of him.

His arms slid over my shoulders, anchoring himself to me. I pushed him back, gently leaning him against the wall behind him. He smiled against my lips, threading his fingers into the back of my hair.

I pulled my lips from his. "Fuck, don't do that." I chuckled.

"You like it when I touch you," he whispered.

"I like it when you touch me anywhere."

His eyes moved past me before he unclasped his hands from around me. He trailed his hand down my arm before he took my hand in his, entwining our fingers. He walked past me and led me out of the lounge and towards my bedroom. Back here there was only the bathroom, my room and a guest bedroom.

He led me to the open door which happened to be my room.

I was shocked at how confident he was being. I believed Sammy when he said he wanted more of us but I was still surprised that this is where we were heading. I know that he was nowhere near ready for the kind of thoughts that were currently running on a loop in my head but the fact that he wanted more of us meant more to me than anything else.

This made me feel like we were moving in the right direction.

He stopped in the middle of the room and gazed up at me.

His face was illuminated by the light from the passage. I could stare into his beautiful green eyes forever. They were deep and they swallowed me whole.

"You're sure about this?" I asked, taking his beautiful face in my hands.

He nodded before a look of hesitation crossed his face. "Small steps?" He sounded certain but he phrased it as a question, almost as though he needed my agreement before moving forward.

I stared into his eyes, needing to get a feel of him before I did something he wasn't ready for.

He may have led me in here but it was clear to me that he was too vulnerable to lead the rest of the way. I had to keep reminding myself that he was vulnerable. If he needed me to lead this, I'd happily do it.

I tilted my head down, wanting his lips on mine. I moved halfway, waiting for him to meet me the other half. He tilted his chin up, offering his lips to mine. I moved the rest of the way, pressing my lips to his softly.

I wanted this man. I'd never tried to hide it from him, but I had been trying to protect him from the depth of my feelings for him—how much I wanted and needed him. I was afraid it would scare him but maybe he needed to know and feel just how much I wanted him.

I slid my arm around his waist and touched my hand on his lower back, pulling his body closer to mine. He relaxed at my touch, winding his arm around my shoulders and urging me closer to him.

I went willingly, loving the feel of him against me. I stepped forward, urging him backward.

His legs hit the back of the mattress and he pulled his lips from mine, chuckling. "You trying to get me into bed?"

I knew he was joking by the cheeky grin that was plastered across his face. I stared at him, silently getting my point across.

He frowned before he stepped back and began kicking his shoes off. Lust stirred through me when he sat down and shuffled his ass across to the middle of the bed before laying down with his head on my pillow.

"Is that better?" he asked, gazing up at me.

I nodded my head before stepping back and kicking my shoes off. I slid on the bed, choosing to lie on my side to make it easier to face him.

"You okay?" I asked, trailing my hand up and down his upper arm.

Tingles shot through my fingers from his touch.

He nodded before whispering, "Kiss me."

I didn't need to be told twice. I moved my face closer to him until we were only centimeters apart. His tongue peeked out to wet his bottom lip and I was done for. Sammy had the power to break me and I didn't think he was fully aware just how much he owned me.

I pressed my lips to his, sucking his bottom lip into my mouth. I groaned at the taste of him, wanting more. Always wanting more.

He parted his lips eagerly, allowing my tongue entry. He moved pressed his tongue against mine, seeking me out.

I could have kissed Sammy for days and not got tired of him.

He slid his hand into the back of my hair.

I tried to ignore the urges moving through me and focus on just his mouth but it was hard. I wanted him anywhere and everywhere all at once.

His hand slid up my side before his other hand moved to my t-shirt covered chest, his fingers twitching and caressing. His hand tightened on the back of my hair before he pulled me with him.

I followed, not able to move my lips from his.

He smiled against my lips before coming back, his hand fisting in the back of my t-shirt.

I slid my arm around him, holding myself closer to him. I pulled moved my lips from his, trailing them across his cheek before pressing small kisses to the column of his neck. He groaned, pushing his head back into the pillows, exposing his neck more to my lips.

I dipped my head lower and licked along the length of his collarbone.

He groaned, his hips lifting off the bed.

A shiver traveled through me when I thought of how hard he was. I was as hard as a rock and I was hoping it was the same for him.

I clenched my hands into fists, shaking my head to

clear those thoughts before moving my lips back to his. The second our lips touched again, we both groaned, tilting our heads to get closer.

"I want you," I whispered, sucking his tongue into my mouth.

"I know." He gasped the words before his hands pressed against my chest, fisting my t-shirt and pulling me against him. He rolled onto his back, pulling lifting my weight to settle more firmly over him.

"What are you doing?" I asked, whispering. What was he doing? This was too fast.

"I want to feel you against me." His lips trailed down, repeating my actions, and he pressed small kisses against the column of my neck.

I groaned at the feel of his lips on my skin and allowed my weight to lower down on him. I was surprised my larger frame fit so well between his legs.

"Does it feel okay?" I asked, wondering what he was thinking.

He nodded, staring into my eyes. I couldn't read the expression for a few seconds. It wasn't fear and it wasn't lust; it was something else—something I had never really seen there before.

He slowly lifted his hips and ground against me before lowering them back to the bed.

I gasped at the feeling. Fuck, he was hard.

I groaned, slamming my lips on his. I held my body up over his, not ready to let it get to that point yet.

I had to remember that this was different with Sammy. Everything was different with Sammy, but this...

This could be so much more.

This could be everything.

NINE
Sammy

Hospitals. I hated them. I had never been a fan ever since I was little but after that episode with Lucy, I hated them more. Seeing Tillie hooked up to those tubes... I don't think any of us will ever forget it.

I stared at the wall in the waiting room, scared shitless. I didn't know why: I'd known this day was coming for a long time but now that it had, I wasn't ready. My leg was bouncing and I couldn't keep my hands still.

"Sammy..." Tillie reached over and took my hand in hers. "It's okay." She enveloped it in hers, trying to calm me.

"I'm scared," I admitted, turning to look at her.

"Of not playing?" she asked. Her eyes briefly flickered past me to where Johnny was standing before coming back to me.

I shook my head negatively. "Of what this will mean for me." I swallowed heavily. "What do I do then?"

Her eyes filled with unshed tears. She knew how important football was to Johnny. Living without it was not an option for him.

My attention was taken when Johnny sat next to me on my other side. He put his arm around my shoulders and pulled me into his side, hugging me close.

"We will manage it, baby brother." He rested his chin on the top of my head, sighing deeply. "We will sort something. Okay?"

I nodded, letting him hug me.

"Sammy Baker." A nurse had stepped into the room and was looking at me with a small smile on her face.

I stood up, squeezing Tillie's hand briefly before following her. Johnny and our coach came with me, which I was glad for. Medical talk usually just flew over my head.

We entered the room and I cringed at how sterile it was. White walls, brown desk, white sheet on the bed.

The doctor was an elderly gentleman and he gave

us a friendly smile before standing up to shake our hands.

"Thank you for seeing us," Johnny said, shaking his hand.

"Not at all. Please take a seat."

There were two seats in front of his desk and the coach and I quickly took them. Johnny chose to remain standing behind me. It was probably a good thing that I couldn't see his face. At the moment, I just wanted to get in and out.

My eyes landed on the brown card folder on his desk that I knew held my notes. He pulled it towards him and took what looked like an x-ray scan out. He turned and placed it on the white screen behind him, lighting it up.

"As you can see," he said, pointing to where my left shoulder was highlighted. "The tear has repaired extremely well and I am happy with the recovery."

There was a 'but' coming. He had ended his sentence in such a way that you knew what was coming. I did, at least.

"That's good, right?" Johnny enthused from behind us.

The coach was silent but his hands were tensed over his knees. He was worried.

"It is very good. Sammy is young and healthy and

I'm happy to say that this will not hold him back. However, I am sorry to have to report..."

I closed my eyes, waiting for it. Over the weeks, I had resolved to be ready and I'd prepared myself as much as I could for the news he was about to deliver.

"I am sorry, Sammy." He took a deep breath before continuing. "I'm afraid the tendons are not as strong as they should be to professionally excel in football."

I nodded automatically, realizing that I may have prepared myself a little too much. I felt nothing at his words. Not relief, not anger. Nothing.

The coach turned to look at me and placed his hand on my shoulder, squeezing.

"I'm sorry, kid." His voice broke and I knew it killed him to receive this news.

I may have only been a reserve, but the coach always treated me as a valued member. He never overlooked the reserves. We were just as important to him as the actual team members.

"Me too." I nodded my head, got up from the seat and shook the doctor's hand.

I walked past Johnny, unable to look at him. I didn't want to see how devastated I knew he had to be. I should have been worried at how little I felt. I just had my dream crushed. Shouldn't I have been feeling something? Something other than relief?

We walked into the waiting room and Tillie stood, a smile briefly appearing on her face before her gaze flicked to Johnny over my head. Her face fell before she looked back to me. She grabbed her bag and linked her arm with mine, giving me a side hug.

I smiled at the sweet action. Tillie was always trying to make others feel better. If you had a problem that she couldn't fix, she'd share it. She gave everything she had to her loved ones. It was no surprise that she and Johnny had gravitated towards each other. They were very much alike.

We filed into the coach's car with Tillie and I sitting in the back. She took my hand in hers and entwined our hands. It was silent the whole way home.

As the car came to a stop, I opened the door but froze when the coach called my name.

"Sammy, come by and see me in a few days, okay?" He looked worried.

I nodded, giving him a small smile. "Sure, boss."

I led the way up to the house, unlocked the door and stepped inside. I didn't bother hanging around downstairs. I didn't want to be forced to talk about it. I wasn't interested in getting second opinions. I just wanted to disappear into my room.

"What are we going to do?" Tillie asked, whispering her concerns to Johnny.

"I don't know, baby girl." He released a deep breath. "I guess we just need to give him his space for now."

I tossed my keys and phone onto my desk and lay on the bed. My eyes landed on the photo of Johnny and me that Tillie forced us to have at practice. We had mud stains all over us but she didn't care.

I turned my body away from it, lying on my side to face the wall.

I felt like a stress ball. I felt like I had been pulled, pushed and squished in too many directions and my elasticity had been stretched out of me.

Football, grades, Benjamin... It had all mounted up until I had nothing left to give.

The sound of footsteps tip-toeing up the stairs made me tense. I wasn't in the mood for questions right now. My door quietly creaked and then I felt the bed softly dip behind me.

I knew it was Tillie before she even entered the room. Like I said before, Tillie was a giver. If she couldn't fix it, she'd help share it.

Her arm slid over my ribs and she hugged herself close to me. She didn't stop until she was basically spooning me. When she touched me, something broke inside of me. It was like her touch had ripped down the wall I had been building up over the last few weeks and now I was nothing but sand and water.

My eyes filled and before I knew it, I was crumbling. I turned my head and cried into my pillow, hating the weakness in me.

Tillie crawled over me and sandwiched herself between me and the wall and crushed her body to mine, tucking her head into my neck, giving me something to cement me and hold me together.

She slid her arm around me and rubbed my back comfortingly. "It's okay, Sammy. It's okay." She paused to sniff and I could feel wetness begin to soak into my t-shirt from her tears. "Let it out. Let everything out."

I did. I listened to her words and let it all come out.

The game, the shooting, Benjamin... I let it all run free and allowed her to hold me.

I woke a few hours later to an empty and darker room. I rolled over and smiled when I saw Tillie had left a glass of milk and one of Joy's famous chocolate chip cookies. She knew my weaknesses all too well.

I took a nibble and reached for my phone, cringing when I saw who I had messages from.

Logan and Benjamin.

I opened Logan's and winced as I read it.

LOGAN

Party tonight at Stella's. Meet you there. We need to celebrate!

I rolled my eyes. Trust Logan to assume that it would be good news. I don't think neither he nor Johnny thought it would come to this.

I didn't bother replying and moved to Benjamin's message.

BENJAMIN

I called earlier and spoke to Tillie. I'm really sorry. Here if you need me.

That message made me smile. Ever since Benjamin had come into my life, he had been nothing but sweet, kind, patient and caring. I was lucky to have him. No matter how confused I got or worried, he'd never rushed me. He'd always been solid and strong.

I grabbed my keys and jogged down the stairs, one direction in mind. I rounded the corner and smiled when I saw Tillie with her feet in Johnny's lap.

"I'm going out, guys."

Johnny's hands tensed on Tillie's feet before he continued rubbing his thumbs against her heel.

"Will you be back later?" "Tillie asked, smiling at me.

"I'm not sure yet." I shrugged my shoulders, not planning that far ahead.

She nodded before she forced a smile back on her face. "Well, have fun!"

They were trying to give me space and make out that everything was okay at the same time. This affected them more than it affected me. They just had to wait and give me time to decide where I went from here. It wasn't the end of me. I just had to figure out what my new reality was going to be.

I made the short walk to Benjamin's, not wanting to be anywhere else. I needed to go. He said he'd be here for me and I believed him. More importantly, I wanted him to be there for me.

I pressed his buzzer and waited impatiently. I hadn't even considered that he may not be there. Before I could fidget too much, his voice echoed through the speaker, calming me.

"Hello." He sounded tired.

"It's me," I replied.

He was silent for a few moments. I fidgeted, starting to worry that maybe I had read too much into his text message. Maybe he was just being polite.

"I was just thinking about you," he confessed.

His voice did things to me no one else's voice had ever done. It warmed and excited me all at once.

The speaker buzzed and the door opened. I jogged up the stairs, equally hating and being thankful for how many floors up he lived as much as I wanted to get there quickly, it gave me that extra bit of time to attempt to calm my emotions.

It didn't work.

As I got to the top of the stairs, I was completely surprised and shocked at the sight that greeted me. Benjamin was leaning up against his doorframe wearing only his gym pants. He had several pieces of ink on his torso and chest.

I smiled when I saw that he had a lily tattooed on him with her name in cursive writing beneath it.

I wanted nothing more than to examine his tattoos up close.

Would he let me? Would it excite him to have me that close to him, noticing the details of the ink engraved beneath his skin?

The sight of him standing there looking sinfully delicious had my knees trembling and the 'come fuck me' smile he was shooting in my direction was my complete undoing.

I marched towards him, eager to be near him and have his hands on me. I roughly pressed my lips against his. He gasped, caught off guard by my actions. He took a step back and I followed him, not stopping until we were both inside.

I kicked the door shut with my foot and allowed him to lean me back against the door. His chest pressed against mine and I groaned at the feel of his hardness against me.

"What are you doing?" he whispered, pulling his lips from mine. He looked into my eyes before pushing the hair back from my forehead. "You're not..."

"I just want to be with you. After today, I just want to switch off and forget about everything out there." I nodded my head to the door, indicating the outside world. "Right now, I just want to forget."

He frowned, looking confused. He looked unsure of what I was asking him.

To be honest, I wasn't sure what I was asking. I just knew that I had to feel something.

He tilted his face closer and touched his lips softly to mine. It was a sweet gesture and one I appreciated more than he knew. He had always been soft and gentle but right now, it wasn't what I wanted.

I lifted my leg and rested it against his hip. I held myself to him and rocked my hips, wanting him to feel me for the first time—wanting him to know just how badly I needed him and I needed him to feel what he did to me.

I gasped as his hand lifted my thigh and moved me harder against him. I knew he was used to having sex on a regular basis and I knew he was wound up tight at being patient for me. For the first time, I wanted what he was offering.

I wanted to know what it felt like to fall apart beneath his touch. With him and only him.

Every time we had been together, he had always been in jeans. Being this close to Benjamin when he was only wearing a thin pair of gym pants was something else completely.

I pressed my lips against his harder, wanting him to be where I was—needing him to want me as crazily as I wanted and needed him.

"You're hard," he whispered. He sounded a little awestruck and surprised.

I pulled my head back and looked into his eyes. "I know."

He moved my leg, placing it back down on the floor before he took a few steps away from me to separate us.

I thought he was pulling away from me at first but then he held his hand out to me.

"Come with me." He sounded so certain, almost as though he knew I wouldn't refuse him.

He was right. I couldn't refuse him.

I stared into his eyes, noticing for the first time that he had tiny specks of gold in his irises. I had never noticed them before.

I must have stared at him for a beat too long when a look of worry crossed his features. I hated seeing it there.

"I won't hurt you," he whispered. "I'll go slow."

I smiled, loving the way he treated me. I never thought I'd ever find what Johnny and Tillie had. That kind of love that no matter what you did, you knew you'd be okay because they'd be there to catch you.

I wanted him to catch me, to want me and for the first time in my life, I wanted someone to need me.

TEN
Benjamin

I offered him my hand, silently asking him to take it. For the first time, I wanted him to see how much I needed him—how much that I had always needed him.

These last few weeks, I had tried to stay in control of my emotions. I'd been afraid they would scare him —afraid that it would be too much and too fast.

As I looked into his eyes, I allowed myself to admit just how special Sammy had become to me. My days started and ended with him. This man had the power to break me and I would never be the same from here on in. It wasn't love that I was feeling for Sammy, but if we kept going in the direction we were heading in, it wouldn't take much.

I was falling fast for Sammy and I didn't want it to stop.

He took a small step forward and reached for my hand. Our fingers entwined and I took a step away, leading him to the bedroom. I know he wasn't ready for us to have sex but I couldn't deny that he was acting more confident, almost as though he was ready for more.

More of us. More of me.

As we walked into the bedroom, I began to get nervous. I had only been with two men before and they were completely different to this. I didn't want to rush this. I couldn't rush this. I had to go slow.

He placed his fingers on my stomach and trailed them up over my chest.

I shivered at the contact, wanting his hands everywhere.

He smiled, before he leaned up, bringing his lips to mine. His hand trailed back down to my stomach before he moved it lower and rubbed my hardness over my pants.

I gasped, pulling back. "Fuck!"

"You want me." He stated it with confidence, as if he was now fully aware just what hold he had over me.

"I do," I whispered.

"Show me." His eyes glistened with lust and uncertainty. "I know you've been allowing me to set the pace but I can't..." He shook his head, as though he didn't know how to explain. "I need you to set the pace in here."

In here? I was confused for a split second before it sunk in. He was in control out there but in this room, he needed me. For our first time at least, Sammy needed to be seduced.

"Come here." I took his wrist in mine and pulled him towards me. "Hold on to me," I said, sliding his arms around my shoulders. I touched my lips to his in a soft kiss before pulling back. "Lie down," I whispered.

He toed his shoes off before sitting on the mattress. He laid down and rested his head on my pillow, staring up at me.

I moved onto the bed and lay down next to him. "Is this okay?" I asked, tucking a strand of hair behind his ear.

He nodded, moving his head closer and pressed his lips back to mine.

I groaned, leaning myself over him, holding my body to his.

His hands trailed over my ribs where they settled. His touch lit me up from the inside and I was eager to know if it'd be the same for him. My thoughts were quickly interrupted when he moved his body and pushed me onto my back suddenly.

"What are..."

Before I could finish my question, he kneeled up and lifted his t-shirt up. My eyes followed the movement. He had a faint happy trail disappearing into his jeans. He was smaller than my frame but he had a fit body.

I groaned, not prepared for what the sight of him being shirtless would do to me. I had fantasized about a shirtless Sammy more than once but the images in my head didn't do him justice. He was perfect.

I must have stared at him like a clueless idiot for a bit too long.

A cheeky grin spread across his face that was downright sinful.

Before he could move, I sat up, wanting to be closer to him. He was kneeling between my legs and all I could think about was how good he looked there.

I took his face in my hands and pulled his lips down to mine, needing them back. Sammy was too fucking sexy and he really had no clue how crazily he had me yearning for him.

He pushed me back to the mattress, settling his weight on top of me. He fit perfectly against me, and as our bodies settled against each other's, he groaned into my mouth, grinding his hips against mine. I moaned at the friction, tilting mine up against his in response. He felt so good with his weight on mine.

"That feel okay?" I asked, rotating my hips again.

"It's g-good," he stuttered, his eyes moving from my eyes to my lips.

"Do you want more?" I asked. I wanted more but I wouldn't just continue without asking.

"M-more?" he asked, not understanding my question. He most likely assumed that I may have been trying to steer this in the direction of sex. Not yet. Not tonight. I had to show him what I was offering.

I moved him back gently until he was lying on his back. I leaned my weight over him and began peppering kisses over his neck.

He groaned, pushing his head back into the pillow and tilting his head to give me better access. He was so responsive to my touch. It was enough to make me come in my pants.

I slid my hand down over his chest, avoiding the scar on his shoulder. I didn't touch it, afraid that it may trigger some bad memories. I didn't want that. I never wanted Sammy to suffer again. He had done enough of that.

He tensed as I laid my hand on his stomach, just above where his jeans were buttoned. Before I could panic that I could be moving too fast, he turned his head towards mine. He slid his hand into the back of my hair and roughly pulled my lips to his.

I loved that he was comfortable enough to be rough with me—to lose control with me.

"Do it," he whispered against my lips before licking the seam of my lips.

I slowly unbuttoned his jeans and slid my hand inside his jeans and boxers. As I moved my hand down, the sound of his zip lowering echoed up to us. I stretched my fingers out, taking his hard length in my hands. I turned my head to look, needing to see him in my hands.

He lifted his hips and pulled his jeans and boxers down a little—not fully, but just enough for his cock to slip free.

I gasped at the feel of him, not expecting his size. I never understood these men that were obsessed with the size of their dicks but Sammy's girth surprised the fuck out of me. I moved my hand slowly up his long length before fisting his head and moving back down.

He moaned, tossing his head back into the pillow.

"That feel good?" I asked. I didn't need his verbal response.

"So fucking good."

I moved my hand up and down slowly and gently

wanting to know what he'd prefer—to learn his body as much as I wanted him to learn mine.

I twisted my hand around the head of his cock, loving the half growl, half moan that came from him.

Sammy was vocal and I fucking loved it. His hands slowly started to wander down my chest until they stopped on the waistband of my pants.

I shook my head and pulled his hand away. "Not tonight."

His face fell at my admission.

If I let him touch me tonight, slow and gentle would go out the fucking window. I'd lose control and I couldn't do that. Not with Sammy. Not ever.

I brought my lips back to his, unable to stop kissing him. He thrust his tongue into my mouth, pulling my chest closer to his.

He had a slight sheen of sweat covering his torso and I wanted nothing more than to follow it with my tongue. Licking and nipping until I could wrap my mouth around his cock.

Would he like it? Would be like my lips around his shaft? Licking and sucking him until there wasn't a drop left?

I wanted to know what he tasted like. I wanted him to lose control and consume me like he had consumed my mind for the past several weeks.

I wanted to be desired by Sammy.

I want to taste you.

"Do it," he whispered against my lips.

My eyes shot open and I stared into his green irises.

Fuck, did I say that out loud?

"You're sure...?"

He had to be sure before I moved this any further than he was comfortable with.

He nodded, not shying away from my gaze.

I stood up and moved to the bottom of the bed. He looked completely fuckable lying there but I shook my head mentally, telling my cock to behave.

I grabbed the end of his jeans and pulled. The force of my pull shifted him a little and he chuckled, grabbing the sheets beneath him and letting me pull his jeans off the rest of the way. I left his boxers on him, wanting him to be comfortable after.

Placing his jeans on the floor, I crawled on the bed until I was lying in between his legs.

I looked up at him, needing to check that he was still okay with this. His eyes reflected back at me with excitement and lust.

"Put your mouth on me," he whispered.

Fuck, Sammy was sexy as hell when he talked to me like that. If he was secretly a dirty talker, I was so fucking screwed. It made me wonder what he'd be like when the time came to us having sex.

I placed my hand at the base of his shaft, shuffling over until my mouth was closer. Moving his cock to my mouth, I started at the base, licking up the side of his shaft.

His eyes closed as he moaned at the sensation. I wasn't sure if he'd ever been sucked off before, but from the sounds coming from him, he obviously liked it.

I licked the side of his shaft before moving my mouth down over him. He was longer than I expected him to be. Moving my mouth up, I licked his head before moving back down.

His hips lifted, moving his cock slowly further into my mouth. "Fuck, that feels good."

He lifted his body into more of a sitting position. As our eyes met, I groaned at the sight of him. He was staring at me with complete lust in his eyes. It made me want to push him back and take his body with mine.

I moved my lips back down him, speeding up my actions slightly. His hips lifted again, causing his cock to move further into the back of my throat.

His hand moved to the back of my hair, moving my head up and down his shaft slowly.

"Is this okay?" he asked hesitantly.

Was it okay? Fuck! His actions were making me want to come in my pants. Sammy's confident side in the bedroom was sexy as fuck.

I nodded my head, fisting my hand around the base of his shaft before I trailed my hand down to his balls. I moved my finger in between them before I moved my mouth down, sucking the left one into my mouth.

He gasped, his hips thrusting off the bed. "Ah, fuck."

I smirked, moving my mouth back to his shaft and lowering my mouth down his cock in faster and firmer strokes.

The sound of his moans increased and I could feel him start to grow harder in my mouth. He was close to coming and I needed it. I needed his taste in my mouth. I wanted to see him when he fell apart.

His head dropped back in a moan.

I tapped his hip, needing his face back on mine. His eyes came to mine and I groaned at how vibrant his beautiful green eyes looked.

"Look at me," I whispered. "I need to see you."

He nodded, shifting his hips to get my attention back to his cock.

I smirked, moving my mouth back. I moved up and down him roughly, sucking him further. His moans increased and I noticed his body was now drenched in sweat.

He grasped my shoulder with his hand, his eyes wide with what looked like worry.

"I'm going to come," he whispered urgently.

I moved my mouth firmer down his cock, indicating my refusal. No fucking way. I scraped my teeth gently along the underside of his shaft, my eyes fixed on his.

That did it.

His mouth opened and the sexiest noise came out of him. Seconds later, he was filling my mouth as he came down my throat.

I groaned at the taste, sucking him further. His chest heaved before he let his arms move, collapsing his weight on to the mattress. I slipped his boxers back over his hips, giving him a little modesty.

I lay down next to him, smiling when he turned over onto his side. His cheeks were flushed and I chuckled at the goofy smile that was currently plastered on his face. I leaned forward and pressed a small kiss to his lips.

"That was..."

"Good? Mind-blowing? Like we should be doing that all the time?" I grinned, teasing him.

"Yes. All of those." He chuckled before moving closer and resting his head on my chest.

I was surprised at the contact. Surprised and awed. Sammy was getting more comfortable when it came to touching me and I loved it. I loved seeing him grow and become comfortable with himself.

I rolled onto my back and held him close. He leaned his head more firmly over my chest and wound his arm around my waist. We both breathed a sigh of relief, as though we both needed the comfort.

"This is nice," he whispered.

I rubbed my hand up and down his back, resting my chin on the top of his head.

"Yeah, it is." I squeezed him tighter to me before continuing. "I may just keep you here."

He smiled briefly before the sound of his phone ringing disturbed our silence. He tensed before he cuddled closer to my chest.

"Is it okay if I stay here tonight?" he asked. "Just tonight." He looked up at me, his eyes glistening with emotion. "Just you and me."

"Of course."

He cuddled back into my chest where we stayed till morning, wrapped blissfully in each other's arms, ignoring the outside world for just a little longer.

ELEVEN

Sammy

Waking up the next day, I groaned, stretching my muscles. Memories of last night flashed through my mind before I turned over, expecting to see Benjamin. The bed was cold so he had obviously been up for a while.

Was he regretting what happened?

I slid off the side of the bed, grabbing my jeans and sliding them on. Leaving the bedroom, I gasped when I smelt the delicious smell of bacon cooking.

I grinned when I entered the kitchen, chuckling at the sight of Benjamin standing at the worktop. He had a batch of pancakes already served up and he was now adding crispy bacon to our plates.

"You're finally awake," he teased, grinning at me.

My eyes trailed down to the ink on his chest before coming back to his face. He looked good with rumpled hair in the morning. It was sexy as fuck.

"Good morning." I walked closer, noticing the tumbler of orange juice on the counter. As I reached for it, so did he.

"I'll do it," he said. "You sit." He pointed his head to the tall chair at the worktop where all the food was sitting. "Dig in."

"So, who are we expecting?" I asked, taking a seat. He had to be expecting company. There was way too much food here for only two people.

"Expecting?" He placed my glass of orange juice on the counter. He had the cutest frown on his face.

"Yeah." I looked up at him. "You've made a lot of food."

Maybe he was expecting his inked family round. I didn't really know. I didn't know much about his daily routine and it bothered me. He had come to know so much about me and I barely knew as much about him. I had to fix that.

He scratched the back of his head, shifting his gaze to the floor. He looked uncomfortable.

"I, uh... I didn't know what you liked." He looked embarrassed that he had now been caught out.

It made me want to just drag him back to the

bedroom and show him just how much I adored this side of him. He continued to surprise me. Just when I thought he couldn't get more perfect, he did something else to demonstrate just how thoughtful he was.

I placed my hand on his hip and pulled him closer so that he was standing in between my parted legs. I pulled his face down to mine and sucked his bottom lip into my mouth. A tremor rolled through him, letting me know just how much he loved my touch.

"It's perfect," I whispered.

He smiled, looking relieved. I wasn't sure if it was more that I didn't think he was crazy for cooking enough food for a dozen people or if it was because I wasn't pulling away from him after last night.

Our relationship hadn't been easy from the start but after the last few days and last night, it had only brought us closer. I was in this with him for as long as he would have me. What was ahead of us was scary but I knew that as long as I had Benjamin, it would be more manageable. His strength would help me to get through it.

I knew that if I wanted a relationship to progress I would have to be more honest. Not only with myself but with my family as well. I was pretty sure that Tillie was already aware of what was going on but Johnny and Logan were a whole other story.

I was ready for more with Benjamin but I wasn't ready to talk to Johnny and Logan. Not yet, at least.

I turned in my seat and stole a rasher of bacon from the plate while Benjamin served a couple of pancakes onto my plate. I moaned at how crispy it was before stealing another one.

He smirked, taking a seat next to me where we ate our breakfast in a comfortable silence.

We spent the rest of the day hanging out in his apartment. I was surprised at how comfortable I felt in Benjamin's arms on the sofa. It felt as though this is what we should have always been doing. Being together was easy and I was already seeing a path for us.

"So," Benjamin said. "How are you feeling?" He sounded hesitant and I was unsure why.

"Feeling?" I turned my head up to his, needing to see his eyes. Benjamin wore his heart on his sleeve and I was worried what he could be thinking.

"After last night," he whispered.

I shook my head, hating that he was worried about last night—hating that he thought I may have regretted it.

"It was perfect," I whispered, not having any other way to explain it.

It was perfect and I wouldn't have changed a thing.

I tilted my chin, silently indicating that I wanted

him closer. He didn't hesitate. He moved his head down as I tilted mine up and brought his lips to mine, softly kissing me. When Benjamin kissed me, he made me feel like the most precious thing in the world.

I wanted to do that for him.

Our moment was disturbed when my phone started vibrating on the coffee table. I cringed, hoping it wasn't Tillie again. She had called me a few times through the night before giving up.

I'm sure she had some serious questions to ask me when I got home.

I frowned when I saw it was Johnny's face flashing across the screen. He never called me.

"Hello."

"Where the hell are you?" He chuckled down the line. "I've been looking for you everywhere."

"I'm hanging out at a friend's house."

I wasn't in the mood to party with the team tonight. Especially not after yesterday.

"Well, they can come too," he teased. "Come on, bro! We haven't had a chance to hang out lately. Plus, I have some good news that can't really be shared over the phone."

"Is Tillie pregnant?" I asked, unable to stop the thrill of excitement that shot through me.

"Fuck no!" he defended. He sighed down the line before continuing. "Don't wish that on us."

I laughed, imagining the look of panic that was probably pasted on his face.

"Where to?" I asked.

I turned to look at Benjamin and chuckled when I saw he was playing Tetris on his phone. I had learned that day that he was fucking obsessed with the game.

"We're at Chunk's," Johnny replied. "Bring your friend with you." He hung up before I could reply.

"We've just been invited to a party." I had gone from calm and chilled to stressed.

"Relax." He put the phone down and took my hand in his. "I can see you stressing already."

I sighed, feeling like a deflated balloon. "Sorry."

"Stop apologizing." He leaned forward and pressed his lips quickly to mine before pulling back. "If you want me to come, I'll come." He shrugged his shoulders. "If you don't want me to, then that's okay, also."

"I want you to come," I whispered, taking his hand in mine.

He smiled before standing from the sofa and pulling me with him. "Let me go and change and then we can go."

I nodded, letting him go. This was going to be interesting.

An hour later, we left Benjamin's and arrived at my house. I left Benjamin in the kitchen as I went upstairs to take a quick shower and change clothes. I opted for my black jeans and my Heath Ledger Joker t-shirt.

I chuckled as I walked into the kitchen and saw that he was eyeing up the plate of cookies that Joy had brought over.

"You can have one." I grinned at him, knowing that he would never look at a cookie the same way after tasting Joy's delicious baking.

He grabbed one and took a small bite.

I turned around to grab my wallet and keys from the lounge and chuckled when I heard a moan slip from him.

"These are fucking amazing!" he gasped, taking another bite. "I need to move in with Joy."

That caused me to laugh harder. I was under the impression that anyone would marry Joy just to get their hands on her cookie recipe. None of us could turn her cooking down.

"You ready to go?" I asked, turning to face him.

He had demolished the cookie and was now standing there staring at me with a sexy smirk on his face. It made me want to drag him upstairs to my room instead of taking him to some boring-ass party as my friend.

He walked closer until we were almost touching. "One more thing." He tilted his head and walked me back until he was pressing me against the wall behind me.

I parted my lips, allowing his tongue entry, needing his taste before this party just as much as he needed mine.

The kiss started off slow and gentle before he pressed his body harder against mine.

I groaned, fisting his shirt and pulling his chest against mine.

"Fuck!" He pulled back and adjusted himself. "Do we have to stay long?" He chuckled.

I giggled, giving him a kiss on the cheek before opening the door. "Just give me the signal and we'll leave."

I was teasing. I think.

During the walk there, I was confused by the feelings coursing through me. I had never really been into public displays of affection but I was struggling. I wanted nothing more than to take Benjamin's hand in mine or have him hold me in some way.

In his apartment, we were always touching in some way or other. I had obviously become accustomed to it. More than that, I obviously liked it—so much that I didn't want it to end.

As we got closer to the house, I distanced myself physically a little more from Benjamin. I couldn't look at him when I did it. I didn't want to see the look of disappointment on his face. I only wanted to see him happy—not disappointed and frustrated with me.

Walking inside, I saw Tillie hysterically waving at me from the corner of the room. She kind of looked like one of those people waving on the Titanic when it left the dock.

I grinned, heading straight for her with Benjamin following me.

She jumped up and wrapped her arms around my neck, her feet lifting off the ground as I hugged her tightly.

"Someone is tipsy." I chuckled, putting her feet back on the floor.

Johnny immediately pulled her back to his side, giving glares to a few of the boys that were looking at Tillie a little too much.

"There he is!" Logan shouted from behind me just

before he threw his arm around my shoulders. "Where the fuck have you been hiding?"

Fucking hell. Was everyone here wrecked?! Johnny seemed to be the only sober one out of them.

"Where's Bex?" I asked, looking around the room.

It was strange for her not to be here. She was usually the life of the party.

"She's out on a date," Tillie chirped up. "So, who is this?" she asked, smiling kindly at Benjamin.

"This is Benjamin." Fuck, now I had to introduce them. "Benjamin, this is Tillie, Johnny and Logan." I pointed each of them out as I introduced them. "Benjamin is a tattooist at Wicked Ink."

Tillie let out a gasp and turned to look up at Johnny.

Benjamin grinned, knowing what Tillie wanted before she even had to voice it. "Do you have any ink?" he asked, directing his question to Tillie.

She shook her head. "I want a drawing of mine tattooed on to my shoulder." She grinned, bouncing on the soles of her feet. "But I am kind of afraid of pain."

Benjamin nodded and moved closer to Tillie, taking a seat next to her. "What about a piercing?" he asked. "Or maybe have a smaller tattoo somewhere else?" He took her wrist and turned it over. "Maybe have something here? It's not as sensitive as the shoulder." He shrugged. "It may give you an idea of how you would handle the discomfort."

I liked that he used the word 'discomfort'. I guess to him it wasn't painful to have ink. He had seen enough customers have tattoos.

He pulled his wallet out and handed Johnny and Tillie both a business card. "Have a think about it and call us anytime. Even if it's just to ask us questions. We're happy to help."

"Thanks, man." Johnny tucked his card into his back pocket and took a swig of his beer.

"So, what's this good news you have to tell me?" I asked. I looked between Tillie and Johnny wondering what it was.

Tillie turned to look at Johnny and I was surprised at how proud she looked. She turned to look at me and placed her hand on Johnny's arm.

"Johnny has some interest from a few scouts." She grinned, knowing just how big this admission was. "A few are going to come and watch him in a few weeks."

"This is fucking amazing!" I grinned, throwing my arms around him and hugging him tightly. I pulled back, letting Logan hug him as well.

"Congratulations, man," Benjamin enthused. He grinned at me before his eyes moved past me.

I turned to look at what had his attention. There was a man standing in the doorway staring straight at Benjamin. He looked our age but I had never seen him before.

Who the fuck was he?!

"Who's that?" I asked, directing my question to Benjamin.

"A-a friend." His tone had turned cold. "I, uh, I had better go and see what he wants."

I nodded, letting him pass and moved into his seat next to Tillie. I sat in silence watching Benjamin follow the guy outside. The conversation continued around me but I was stewing in jealousy and anger.

Where the fuck had he gone?

Tillie kept flicking her gaze to me. I could tell she wanted to say something but she couldn't really, considering she was sandwiched in between Johnny and me.

My phone vibrated with a text message from Benjamin:

BENJAMIN

Sorry. I had to leave. Problem with Lily. She needs me right now.

"Is everything okay?" Tillie asked, her gaze flicking down to my phone.

"Yeah." I slipped the phone back into my pocket. "He had a personal problem he had to sort."

She nodded, linking her arm with mine and resting her head on my shoulder.

I stayed there for the next hour, staring at the door and not even bothering to join in on the festivities and have a drink.

An hour later, we began the walk home with a wobbling Tillie. The girl could never handle her booze.

I pulled my phone out and called Benjamin. The phone rang several times but he never picked up. I shook my head in frustration, before dialing Lily's number, hoping to leave a message for Benjamin.

"H-hello." She sounded groggy. "Sammy? Is that you?"

"Uh, yeah. Is everything okay?"

I frowned, confused. She didn't sound upset or worried.

She giggled. "You called the wrong number, sweetie."

"No." I sighed. "We were at a college party earlier and he left saying that he had to sort out a problem?" I ended it as a question, feeling unsure.

I was feeling unsure of everything now.

"I thought he might have been there with you."

"No, sweetie. He's not here." She sighed before continuing. "Maybe he went straight home?"

"Yeah, maybe." Why would he lie to me? "Sweet dreams, Lily."

I hung up and entered the house behind Johnny and Tillie. After locking up, I switched the lights off and lay down on my bed.

What the fuck was going on?

TWELVE
Benjamin

Hanging out with Sammy and seeing him around his friends and family was better than I thought it would be. It was plain to see just how close Tillie and Sammy were. There was a bond there that made them family.

It was special.

This family was made of more of a deeper connection than blood. Love, loyalty and passion tied them together and I loved seeing Sammy in the center of that group. He was lucky to be a part of such a close-knit bond and I was honored that he thought enough of us to introduce me to them.

As I stood there and watched his enthusiasm and excitement for Johnny's good news, you'd never think that only yesterday Sammy had lost his chance to play football as a profession. He was genuinely happy for his brother and there was no animosity there. Just love.

Love and acceptance.

As I looked at Sammy, I knew that it was exactly where I should be. My path had led me to Sammy and I was right where I was needed.

I looked past Sammy and froze at the sight of him standing in the doorway.

Charlie. My worst mistake.

Sammy turned to look at what had my attention. "Who's that?" he asked. There was an edge to his voice that had never been there before. He sounded jealous.

"A-a friend," I stammered. The lie rolled right off my tongue before I could stop it. "I, uh, I had better go and see what he wants," I mumbled.

I was ashamed. I hated liars and had vowed to never become one and now here I was, lying to the one person I thought that I was most certainly falling in love with.

I moved past him, cringing the closer I got to him. I was not in the mood for whatever fucking mind game this douchebag had in mind. My life was as close to perfect as it could and I did not need this fucker coming in and screwing it up.

Charlie used to be a friend. A few years ago, we

had been as close as Logan and Sammy were. I thought that he was the most genuine person until I learned that he wasn't. He had taken my wallet, the cash I had kept in my cookie jar for emergencies and he had also broken into Wicked Ink and trashed the place.

He smiled as I approached but I didn't stop. I began walking away and leading him from the party. Charlie and my life with Sammy would not mix well and I didn't want him infecting Sammy's life. He had been through so much and he didn't need Charlie's poison leaking into it.

I sent a quick message to Sammy, not wanting him to worry or wait for me to come back. I hated lying to him again but I needed time to explain this fuck up in person. Not right then.

The further away we got, the angrier I became. I wasn't sure if I was more angry at him for thinking he could just walk back into my life or at myself for not making it clear previously that he wasn't welcome here. Not in this town or in my life.

"How have you been, man?" he asked. He was obviously trying to play the 'friend' card but not today. I wasn't in the fucking mood.

"I haven't seen you in over a year." Was he fucking crazy? "You stole from me, ransacked my business and thought we would... what? Just pick up from where we left off."

His lip curled in disgust, as he turned his glare on me.

"What the fuck do you want, Charlie? Run out of money?"

"Seriously?" he scoffed. "I've seen the shop, man. You're doing well for yourself."

"Yeah, I am," I said, nodding my head. "And I don't have time for you."

Before I could blink, he punched me in the face, knocking me backward. I reached out, grabbing on to the wall to stop going down. I spun around to face him and threw myself at him, wrapping my arms around him and taking him down to the ground.

I wrestled with him, not stopping until I was on top of him. I raised my fist but before I could deliver it, his hand wrapped around my clenched fist and he slammed his head against mine.

I toppled to the side, rolling off him. I felt two sets of hands grab my arms and hoist me up until I was standing. I groaned, not liking the cocky smirk that was plastered across his face. The two men holding me up held me tighter while Charlie began delivering blow after blow on my face and ribs.

When he was finished, they threw me to the

ground. Looking up at the stars, I curled into a ball, trying to ease some of the pain in my ribs.

Charlie leaned over and grasped my face in his hand, squeezing my cheeks roughly.

"I don't need you," he spat. "I'm better than you."

I cringed as he squeezed tighter.

"You'll regret this." Another kick to the ribs. "You and your precious fucking, Sammy."

He punched me in the face once more. I lay back on the ground, cringing at the pain. I closed my eyes, unable to keep them open as darkness quickly followed.

———

I groaned at the feeling shooting through my ribs. I could feel myself being jostled between two people, my feet dragging behind me. I had an arm around each person and I had no clue who the hell they were. My left eye was swollen shut and I could taste blood in my mouth.

"I think he's waking up," a female voice chirped up on my right.

I groaned, my head lolling to the side so that I could look at her. She was a pretty girl and had long blonde hair.

"Thank fuck for that!" a male voice sounded to my left.

I turned to see who it was as the voice sounded very familiar. He was blurry thanks to my left eye but I couldn't mistake who it was.

Logan.

Fuck my life!

"What happened, man?" he asked. He tightened his grip on my arm, hoisting me up a little more. "Was on my way home when I found you passed out on the ground."

I shook my head, not knowing what to say. "I had a disagreement with someone."

He cocked an eyebrow at me, not believing me.

"Just take me home, please."

He was shaking his head before I even had the words out. "No fucking way, man. I'm taking you to Sammy."

"No!" I refused. "You can't take me there."

Fuck, if he saw me like this, it would scare him. There were good people in this world and I didn't want the sight of me beaten to a pulp scaring him further into the closet. He had a good life and a good family around him. He was better off than other people in this situation.

Logan looked at the lady on my right before he shook his head, rolling his eyes.

"Fine! We'll take you to Bex's. It's closer."

I nodded, thankful that I wouldn't have to face Sammy.

The day had started out so perfectly and now it had all gone to complete fucking shit.

After getting to Bex's apartment, I was dumped on her bed. Bex was a sweetheart. She cleaned the cuts and scrapes on my face before they helped remove my t-shirt. She wrapped some bandages around my ribs after Logan gave me a quick examination. He didn't think they were broken but they were definitely bruised.

I lay there, trying to take small breaths before their whispers from the doorway started.

"Is he going to be okay?" Bex asked. She didn't try and hide the worry in her tone. She wasn't stupid. She knew an ass-kicking when she saw one.

"Yeah, he'll be fine," Logan replied. "He's just going to have to take it easy."

His phone began ringing before he stepped away.

Minutes later, he was back, sounding pissed off. "I have to go. There's a problem I need to sort out."

"Problem?" Bex asked, her voice fading away as she walked him out.

I stared at the wall, feeling numb.

How the hell was I going to get out of this?

More importantly, how the hell was I going to keep these bruises from Sammy?

A few hours later, silence had descended upon the apartment. I sat up slowly, cringing at the pain in my ribs. I looked across the room and saw Bex curled up in the chair by the window with a blanket over her.

I grabbed my discarded t-shirt from the end of the bed and slowly pulled it toward me. I made sure to stay as quiet as possible, not wanting to disturb Bex. I knew she'd have questions if I woke her.

I slowly snuck out and left her apartment complex, beginning my walk home. It took me longer than it normally would have but as soon as I got home, I stripped and climbed into the shower.

The water beat down on my sore muscles and relieved some of the tension there.

The bandages that Bex had placed around my shoulders hadn't really done much to ease the ache there and I wouldn't be surprised if one or two of the ribs were broken.

After drying, I slid my sweatpants on and climbed into bed. My phone beeped and I groaned as I reached for it.

One text message from Lily.

LILY

"Sammy called me. You have a personal problem? What's going on?"

I sighed a deep breath, placing the phone back on the side, not even bothering to reply.

What was going on? Fuck if I knew. All I knew was that trouble had just rolled back into town and had come straight for me.

The next morning, I woke up to a loud and incessant banging on my door. I sat up slowly, groaning at the aching ribs and pounding in my head.

"Benjamin Daniels! Open this door!"

Fucking hell. Lily had no idea how to be quiet.

I hobbled to the door and no sooner had I opened it was she forcing her way inside.

She stormed past me and marched into the lounge, turning and tapping her foot. Her face fell when I turned to her. She ran towards me, reaching her hand up to trace around my eye.

"What happened?" She looked less angry and more visibly upset now.

I pulled away, moving past her and taking a seat on the sofa. I held my ribs on the left side, trying to take smaller breaths.

"Charlie is back in town," I replied, not needing to explain any further.

"Why?" She looked angry. "Didn't he take enough from us last time he was here?"

I took her hand in mine, trying to offer her some comfort. I often forgot that he didn't just hurt me last time: he also hurt my family.

She sighed, looking at my bruises. "He had help, didn't he?"

I nodded, looking away from her.

"If it had been one on one, you would have laid him out."

She was right. He wouldn't have had a chance. One on one, it would have been over before it had started.

"So, what happens now?" she asked. She was worried.

Last time he'd been in town, we'd had to close for two months and get a loan to replace all our equipment. He hadn't just stolen from our safe: he had completely wrecked everything in the shop.

Before I could answer, she was asking her next question. "Why did you lie to Sammy?"

I shrugged, not knowing what to say. "Things are good with Sammy." I frowned. "For the first time, Sammy is more comfortable with the idea of 'us'." I swallowed, hating the lump that had formed in my throat. "What if I lose him?"

Lily reached over and placed her index finger beneath my chin. She turned my face to hers and I hated the sympathy that was written on her face.

"If you lie to him, you will lose him, sweetie."

I nodded, knowing she was right.

I hated liars. I never understood them and now I had slowly started becoming like them. They may not have been big lies but they were lies all the same. I had spent so many weeks building a trusting and honest relationship with Sammy and I was now gambling that away by not being truthful with him.

"Get some rest today and go and see him tomorrow." She squeezed my hand before getting up and walking to the door. She opened the door and turned back to me before leaving. "Don't leave it too long, though. He doesn't seem like a very patient man when he wants something."

She slipped out and closed the door, leaving me alone with my thoughts.

I stayed on the sofa for the next hour, not wanting to move—not wanting my ribs to feel like I would be wedging a concrete block between them.

I rolled my eyes at how pathetic I was being and pulled myself off the sofa, cringing at the pain as I made my way to the kitchen.

I jumped in shock when someone knocked on the front door loudly. I stood still, afraid to even breathe. I knew who it was before his sweet voice even came through the door.

"Benjamin?" he called. "Are you there?"

I remained silent, not ready. I would force myself to talk to him tomorrow but not right now.

If Sammy saw me, I was scared he would get scared and run. I would lose him again and I wasn't ready for that. I wasn't ready to admit defeat.

The sound of my phone ringing came from the bedroom. I made sure not to move, letting it ring and go to voicemail.

"Please open the door." He sounded afraid. "Whatever happened last night... I'm sorry if something made you feel that you had to leave. Or that I won't understand."

He sounded like he was going to cry and it made me feel like even more of a monster.

"If something happened, we can talk about it. I know you wouldn't hurt me. So, please open the door and stop me from thinking the worst."

I closed my eyes, fighting past the lump in my throat.

"Please, Benjamin, just open the door."

I didn't move. I didn't make a single noise to alert to him that I was here.

I just stood there like a pathetic moron, waiting for Sammy to walk away.

THIRTEEN
Sammy

Walking away from Benjamin's I felt like even more of an idiot than when I'd arrived. I knew he was home. There was nowhere else he could be. Wicked Ink didn't open for another two hours and he wasn't at the skate park. There was nowhere else I could think to check for him.

I stood outside his building and looked up at his window just in time to see his curtains twitch.

I let my head drop in disappointment.

What had I done? Had I moved too fast? Should I have held off on introducing him to my world?

I shook my head. No. It was fine. He was fine.

At least until that stranger turned up. The second

Benjamin saw him he had turned cold. He had become almost a stranger to me.

My Benjamin was sweet and kind and gentle. Not cold and dismissive.

Was he the reason that Benjamin didn't want to let me in? Were they in there together?

No! I refused to even think it. He wouldn't do that to me.

I walked past the house, not wanting to go back in just yet. I couldn't take the way Tillie kept looking at me. She knew there was something wrong and I could see she just didn't know what to say. Especially with Johnny hanging around.

I hated that she'd figured it out and I hated it more if it was putting a strain on her. She didn't deserve that.

I walked towards the college and headed for the field. It would be the first time I'd been back there since meeting with the doctor.

I chuckled when I saw the coach sitting on the bottom row of the bleachers.

"Hey, coach."

His head shot up before grinning at me. "Hey, kid." He tapped me on the shoulder as I sat next to him. "I thought you had forgotten about us."

I shook my head. "I just needed some time to myself, I guess."

He nodded, not arguing. "I can understand that." He looked back to the field before noting some plays down. He always had that clipboard in his hands.

"Johnny would be better passing to Chunk."

He smirked before looking up at me. "And why would you say that?"

"This is for the next game, right?" I cocked an eyebrow at him, waiting for his reply.

He nodded.

"Well, they are going to go straight for Johnny if he's that far up the field. If he passes to Chunk, it will free him up a little and divert their attention. He can then get up the field a little more and Chunk can then pass him the ball."

Before I had even finished talking, he was scribbling his lines out and drawing more arrows to indicate the play I had just described.

"We're going to miss you around here, kid." He tapped my knee before getting up. "Don't be a stranger." He pointed his pencil at me before he turned around and began walking to the exit.

I made my way to the changing rooms, realizing that I had forgotten to check if my locker was cleared out. Walking in, I switched the light on, cringing when I saw my locker still had my name on it. I opened it and laughed when I saw I had only my hoodie inside with the team logo on. I took it out and slipped it on before peeling my sticker off. I tossed it in the bin and took a seat on the bench, leaning my back against the locker and staring across the room at the glass trophy cabinet in the corner.

I'd stared at it dozens of times over the last few months and I had memorized every single frame in that cabinet. I was surprised to see the top shelf that was normally bare had a frame in it. Every other shelf had a trophy and a frame inside but the top shelf had only a frame.

Walking closer, I grinned when I saw that it was a picture of the coach's current team. He'd made sure that on the first day of training, he got the whole team together—including the reserves— for one group picture. We'd all fussed and rolled our eyes at how sappy he was being but thinking back on it now, maybe it was meant to be.

It was nice to see.

My eyes landed on Johnny in the photo and he looked so proud. He had his arm slung around my shoulders and he looked genuinely happy—like he was right where he needed to be.

Stepping away from the cabinet, I froze when I turned around and saw I had a guest.

An unwanted one.

"Hello, Sammy." He smirked at me before he took a step further into the room.

"Hello." He stared at me and it was pissing me off. "I'm afraid I don't know you."

"I'm Charlie." His grin stretched wider across his face. "I'm a friend of Ben's."

"Ah, I see." I walked past him, leaving the building. "I had better be going."

"I'd like to have a word with you, if you don't mind," he called after me.

I continued walking, my pace increasing. Like fuck was I talking to him. If I had to talk to anyone, I'd rather it be Benjamin standing here. Not some asshole I know fuck all about.

"I'm sorry I had to keep your boyfriend from you last night." He sounded so fucking cocky.

I spun around wanting to lay him out. I was not in the fucking mood for this.

"We had a lot of catching up to do, if you know what I mean."

"Not really." I smiled at him, trying to show that his words didn't bother me. Even though they did bother me a whole fucking lot.

"We're just friends." I shrugged my shoulders refusing to play this sick little joke of his.

"So, you guys haven't spoken?" He took a step closer. "Well, that is very awkward."

I really didn't like the tone he was using. He was using a sickly sweet tone and it was really starting to bother me.

My eyes darted to behind him where I saw four boys walking up in our direction. I didn't recognize them. They weren't members of this team. I heard the scuffle of feet against concrete and saw another four boys walking up behind me.

This was not fucking good.

Living with Johnny, I had been taught how to throw a punch and how to take one. One-on-one I could do, but this was not going to be one on one.

Before I could turn back to ask Charlie what the fuck his problem was, his words stopped me dead, causing anger to flow through my body.

"You see, Benjamin really pissed me off last night by saying shit he had no right to be saying." He cracked his knuckles, letting the silence fester. "I had to teach him a lesson." He smirked, knowing full well what reaction his words were going to cause. "So, me and my buddies laid him out on the ground where we left him."

"You're lying," I seethed.

I looked down at his hands and saw a few of his

knuckles were bruised. I was going to fucking kill him. I took a step toward him before I was lurched forward when I was hit on the back of the head by something really fucking heavy.

I stumbled forward, not appreciating that fucking hit. I touched my hand to the back of my head and cringed when I felt wetness. Pulling it back to see, I knew it would be red before I saw it.

I looked up, my eyes landing on Charlie. Before I could move towards him, my arms were grasped in a tight vice from behind me by two of his boys. Charlie walked towards me but before he could get too close, I kicked my feet out and hit him in the chest.

He stumbled back and came at me again. Before I knew what was happening, he began slamming his fists into my face.

I had been in many fights before and this wasn't like any of them. I could often get an odd punch in here and there but right now, my face was a punching bag for Charlie to pound his aggression and anger out on.

The only thing that was registering around me was the snickering and calls for Charlie to punch the faggot harder. I spat some blood out, feeling one of my teeth go with it. I looked up just in time to see Charlie nod his head towards a boy to the right before

I was hit from the side with a rather large plank of wood.

The last thing I saw before darkness descends— before I closed my eyes, letting the pain pull me down —was Charlie and his team looking down at me.

FOURTEEN
Tillie

I walked to the window for what felt like the twentieth time in the last half hour. Peeking through the curtains, I looked out, waiting for Sammy. He was usually home by now or he would at least pick up his phone when I called.

I wouldn't have been so worried if I hadn't already spoken to Benjamin, but he had answered his phone when I rang after stealing it from the business card he had handed Johnny. Sammy wasn't with him and he didn't know where he was.

So, where the hell was he?!

"Tillie, stop pacing."

I turned my head to Johnny and sighed. "But where is he?" I sounded like a whiny cheerleader.

"I'm sure he's at a party with Logan or something." He gave me a cheeky smile before continuing. "That's what single guys usually do when they are in college, baby girl."

I took a seat next to him and rested my head against his shoulder.

"It doesn't feel right," I whispered. "The last time I felt like this was when Lucy was in here."

I cuddled myself closer to Johnny, hating the ice cold feeling that ran through me.

He slid his arm around me and lifted my face to his, pressing a quick kiss to my lips.

"That will never happen again, sweetheart."

He looked into my eyes and I knew that he was being truthful. He would always protect me.

"Do you want to go and look for him?" he asked.

It was past 10pm but I nodded my head, getting up and grabbing a coat. I quickly slid my sneakers on and took Johnny's hand that reached out to me and followed him out the door.

We walked past Benjamin's and through the skate park but there was no sign of him. We then made our way towards campus when Johnny began leading me towards the stadium. We walked through the entrance and saw that the lights were on in the changing room block down the other end of the field.

As we walked closer, I frowned, feeling a sharp spike of panic begin to settle in my chest. We sped up our pace and ran further ahead. I cringed when I saw the damage that had been done to the bleachers and the block. Some of the seats had been ripped from their places and others were spray painted with offensive graffiti.

I turned my head to look at Johnny and I cringed at how angry he looked. Homophobic insults were spray painted all over the changing room block. That feeling I'd had in my gut all evening began to fester and tightness spread across my chest.

"I'm going to fucking kill them," Johnny threatened.

"We need to find Sammy!" I demanded.

I was scared for Sammy. These insults could only be aimed at one person on this team and I was terrified what they would do to Sammy if they got their hands on him.

Johnny looked down at me, staring at me for a few moments.

At first, I thought he was going to question me—ask me things that I couldn't answer. Before I could worry too much about that, he nodded his head and took a step toward the building.

We walked in and I cringed at the graffiti inside.

Every surface was covered and the coach's prized trophy cupboard was smashed to pieces. Even the trophies were damaged.

I wanted to cry. These items were so important to the coach. It was his legacy and they had ruined it.

"Don't cry, baby girl." Johnny pulled me into his chest and stroked his hand up and down my arm. "Trophies don't make a team."

He knew how important those trophies were to the coach. He knew they couldn't be replaced but he was trying to be positive. It was one of the many reasons why I loved him.

"Stay here and I'll go and check the showers." He pressed a kiss to the top of my head before walking away.

I sighed, taking a seat on the bench and faced away from the cabinet in tatters. I couldn't bear to look at all those years of hard work lying in a smashed heap. I leaned back against the locker behind me when Johnny's voice called me.

"TILLIE!" He screamed my name and I could hear the panic in it.

I shot to my feet and ran in his direction, terrified of what I was walking into.

I came around the corner and froze, a sob escaping me when I saw them. "Sammy!"

Sammy was propped against the wall. He was soaked from the showers being directed to him and there was blood. So much blood.

"Call an ambulance!" Johnny shouted.

I pulled my phone out, dialing 911.

"Emergency services. How may I help?" a calm and professional female voice said.

"I need an ambulance," I sobbed. "My friend... he... he's..." My hand shook as I tried staying calm. "My friend was beaten up and he has... he has blood on him..."

After telling her that he had a pulse and where we were, she told me that an ambulance was on its way.

I hung up and slid down to my knees on Sammy's other side. I was afraid to touch him. He wasn't alert enough to hold himself up. I looked up at Johnny and sobbed when I saw how tightly he was holding Sammy.

He held him, leaning his body against his and stroking his hand through the back of his hair.

"It's okay, Sammy." He choked, the tears reflecting in his eyes. "It's going to be okay." He looked at me and I could see that the man I loved was breaking and there was nothing I could do to fix it.

What felt like minutes later, EMT's were walking in with their equipment.

Johnny knew better than to get in the way. He slowly

laid Sammy down on the cold and wet ground before he stood back. He pulled me into his chest, hugging me tightly while we watched the EMT's check Sammy over before lifting him and placing him on a stretcher.

They lifted him up into the ambulance and attempted to shut the doors.

"Wait!" Johnny called stepping forward. He gripped my hand, pulling me with him. "I'm his brother."

The younger EMT nodded. "Only one is allowed."

Johnny looked down at me before I placed my hand on his back, giving him a gentle push forward. "Go."

He dipped his head, giving me a quick kiss. "Come and find me in the waiting room."

He quickly climbed into the ambulance and it slowly pulled away.

I turned to run in the opposite direction, only one location in mind. I ran through several side streets until I got to Wicked Ink. I was happy the lights were on as I pushed the door open. I gasped for breath when I reached the counter, surprising the girl sat behind it.

"Can I help you?" She didn't look impressed.

"I need Benjamin," I gasped.

"Sorry, sweetie, he's not working today." Her eyes

flicked behind me where there was now a man standing with ink on his arms. "Can Tyler help?"

The man stepped forward and gave me a friendly smile, eyeing me in much the same way that the girl behind the counter was.

"No." I shook my head. "I need Benjamin."

She frowned before she came around the counter. "Who are you, lady?"

"I'm a friend of Sammy's. There's been an accident. Sammy has been taken to the hospital. I need Benjamin."

Her eyes narrowed at me, probably speculating how I knew to come here before her expression cleared and she walked past me. She grabbed her coat off the hook before she turned to Tyler.

She gave him a pointed look as we passed and led me from the shop. "He'll be at home," she said, turning to me. "Let's go."

We left the shop and quickly made our way to Benjamin's apartment complex An older gentleman held the door open for Lily before she led us up a few flights of stairs.

She banged on the door loudly but even after several attempts of knocking and yelling through the door, there was no answer.

Fuck, where the hell was he?! I didn't have time for this. "I thought you said he'd be here."

"You try." She waved her hand towards the door and cocked an eyebrow at me.

Was she serious?

I marched forward and slammed my palm against the door.

"Benjamin!" I yelled through the door. "It's Tillie!"

No answer.

I looked at Lily and groaned in frustration when she waved her hand, getting me to continue.

"It's Sammy!" I yelled, continuing the shouting. "He's had an accident and he's..."

I was sharply cut off when the door swung open and Benjamin stood in the occupied space. I gasped as I looked up at him, mortified when I saw bruises on his face and his left eye was swollen nearly shut.

"What happened?" he asked, demanding some answers.

"He was attacked." My eyes filled with water and it was useless to stop them. "We found him passed out and he... he had blood... and there were so many vile things graffitied on the floor... and I... and he..."

I was openly sobbing at this point, not making any sense at all.

Before I knew it, I was pulled forward and cocooned in a tight hug before he pushed me gently back and turned to grab his coat.

"Let's go."

I nodded, turning away and jogging down the stairs, leading them back out into the open. We piled into Benjamin's car and he drove us the rest of the way to the hospital. Everyone was dead silent with only one person on each of our minds.

I sent a quick text to Logan, needing him with me.

LOGAN

Get to the hospital. There's been an accident. Sammy needs us.

FIFTEEN
Benjamin

When Tillie turned up at my door with Lily, I had every intention of ignoring them. I didn't need this. I just needed time to myself to get my head clear and form a plan. I didn't have any idea how to fix this colossal fuck up and keep Sammy out of it.

The banging started on the door before Lily's voice started yelling. I loved her but the girl did not really have a clue when someone wanted to be on their own. I rolled my eyes, determined to ignore it. She'd get the message eventually.

She gave up after a few more bangs on the door before a few moments of silence passed. Then Tillie's voice called out to me, flipping my world and turning everything upside down.

The second I opened the door, I wanted to scream at the emotion I could see reflected in her eyes. She looked broken and I knew it was bad.

I didn't hesitate in following her out of the building and driving to the hospital.

As we arrived, I passed my keys to Lily and told her to drive it home. I wouldn't be needing it tonight.

Tillie marched straight up to the reception counter and Lily took my hand in hers and entwined our fingers, squeezing gently.

"I'm here to see Sammy Baker," she said. "He was brought in by an emergency ambulance. I'm his sister."

"The doctors are with him at the moment," she replied, giving Tillie a small smile. Take a seat in the waiting room and as soon as there's news, someone will be right out."

Tillie's shoulders slumped before she turned and led us down the hallway to the waiting room. Due to how late it was, the room was mostly empty. She took a seat in the first row of empty seats. I took a seat next to Tillie. She looked like she was falling apart.

The next hour slowly passed; visitors came and went and one by one, we were the last ones in the room. I stared at the clock as the hands slowly moved. It made me want to rip the fucking thing off the wall.

Tillie shot to her feet when Logan walked into the

waiting room. He looked frantic and scared. Logan pulled her into a bone-crunching hug. She was crying into his chest and I knew this situation tonight was too fresh in their minds. Last time, it had been Tillie lying in a hospital bed and now here they were again, waiting for news of a loved one.

"What happened?" Logan asked, still holding her.

She pulled back, wiping her eyes before pulling him down into the seat next to her. She took his hand in hers before leaning over and taking mine.

I gave her my full attention, needing these details just as much.

"Sammy didn't come home and I was getting anxious. He wasn't picking up his phone and I..." She shook her head, sighing. "Johnny and I went looking for him and found him at the field." Her eyes filled once again with tears and they slowly trickled down her face. "We found him in the showers and he was... he wasn't... He had blood on him and his—" She shook her head again, gripping my hand tighter. "He wasn't moving."

I turned away, feeling hate burn through me at her admission.

I had done this. I had brought this vileness into their lives.

"This is my fault," I whispered. I let go of her

hand, letting my head drop between my knees. "If I had stayed away, if I'd never approached Sammy..."

Tillie placed her hand on my shoulder. "Benjamin..."

I shook her off, not needing her comfort. I didn't deserve to be made to feel better. I didn't want and I didn't need it. We were all here waiting for news on Sammy because my asshole of a friend used him as a punching bag to get a message across. I'd made Sammy believe that he would never be hurt like I had been when I came out because he had a good family and now...

Now he was lying in a fucking hospital bed awaiting medical care.

"What do you mean?" Logan asked with a no-nonsense attitude. "Is this to do with what happened to you a few nights ago?" He looked pissed. At me or at the person that did it, I wasn't sure.

"My friend Charlie did this." I was disgusted to even use the word 'friend'.

I avoided looking at Tillie, unable to look at her sweet and trusting face. I didn't deserve for her to look at me like that.

"Why?" Logan looked angry.

His fists tensed at his sides and I could see just how

much he would love to lay me out on this floor. I would let him. I deserved every bit of his anger.

"Charlie lived here and he needed money. I didn't have it to give. Everything I had was tied up in the shop." I shook my head, not needing this trip down memory lane right now. "Long story short, he stole my wallet, trashed the shop and took our savings from the safe."

"So, he's come back looking for another handout."

I nodded my head, avoiding his gaze.

"I still don't see why they would attack Sammy," Logan said, turning to look at Tillie.

She subtly shook her head at him before looking past me.

"Johnny!" She ran to him, wrapping herself in his arms. "How is he?"

He frowned, sliding his arm around her waist and walked past me. He slumped down in his seat, pulling Tillie down so that she was sitting sideways across his legs.

"He's okay." He released a sigh of relief, pulling Tillie further into his arms. "He was unresponsive when they brought him in. He has a slight concussion and they'd like to keep him in for the night. They've given him some pain medication and he's sleeping now."

"Has he asked for anything?" Tillie asked, lifting her head to gaze at Johnny.

Johnny's eyes flicked to me, making me cringe. I knew Logan didn't know but I wasn't sure if Johnny was aware of Sammy's and mine relationship and to be honest, I really didn't want to be the one to tell him. It should be Sammy.

"Benjamin."

Tillie looked over at us, a look of confusion on her face.

"He asked for Benjamin," he continued, elaborating on the reason for saying my name.

It filled me with hope and sadness that he'd asked for me: sadness that I'd brought this on him and hope that it meant something.

I had fallen hard for Sammy and I was foolish enough to dare to hope that he felt the same.

"Can I... can I go and see him?" I asked. I tried keeping the desperate edge from my tone but I don't think I succeeded.

Tillie gave me a small smile before Johnny nodded.

"Sure, go on in."

I all but ran from the room, desperate to see him—eager to know just what kind of shape he was in. The nurse was already there at his door, holding the door open for me.

"I'll give you both a few minutes alone." She gave me a small and sympathetic smile before she closed the door.

He was in a private room and propped up on the bed. There was dim lighting due to it being past midnight but it was still light enough for me to see the damage that Charlie and his asshole friends had done to him.

I'd gotten off lightly in comparison.

He had a few bruises on his face and neck and a deep cut right across the center of his forehead near his hairline. I wouldn't be surprised to learn if they'd continued pummelling him after they had knocked him out. Charlie had never been a fair fighter and it was obvious that he had let a lot of his aggression and anger out on Sammy.

I took a few steps forward and sat next to him on the bed. I could feel a knot form in my chest when I saw the bruises on his knuckles. It broke me at the thought of him trying to fight them off. I imagined him being brave and staring them down, determined not to show them how afraid he really was when in reality, he was most likely very scared and knew just how outnumbered he was.

That was my Sammy though. He was a fighter.

I placed my hand on his, hating how cold his skin

was. I kept imagining him lying in those cold and damp shower cubicles, just waiting for someone to come and find him. I laid my head down on his hand, feeling everything come undone.

I let the tears fall, knowing full well that this couldn't be fixed. If I lost Sammy because of this, I didn't know how I'd be able to walk away from him. I felt that what we had was as damn fucking near to perfect as I would ever get.

Sammy was it for me and now I was convinced that after all of this, I was going to lose him.

I felt someone walk into the room behind me before a small pair of hands rested on the tops of my shoulders and then wrapped around my chest. Seconds later, I felt a small body hug themselves close to me, squeezing me gently before rocking us from side to side.

"He's going to be okay," Tillie whispered, continuing her rocking motion, attempting to soothe us both.

I nodded in response to her words, not having any of my own in response.

The nurse allowed each of us to have some time with Sammy before she put her foot down and kicked us from his room. When it was Logan's turn to sit with Sammy, he only stood by the door and watched him.

The nurse told us to go home but Johnny and I both refused. Logan and Bex left for the night and Tillie cuddled up on the row of seats with her head resting on Johnny's leg. He took her hand in his, twisting the ring on her finger back and forth. It was plain to see they were in love.

When Sammy had said that he and Tillie were close, I had underestimated just how close they actually were.

I sat in the corner of the room, staring out of the window most of the night. Sleep evaded me and my mind just wouldn't shut down. My heart knew that Sammy was going to be okay but my mind would just refuse to stop running.

Hours later, I was being poked awake by Tillie with a cup of tea and a donut. She reminded me a lot of Lily. They both appeared to be kind and caring and always putting other people first.

"How did you sleep?" she asked, looking at me with concern.

I shrugged my shoulders dismissively. "Is he awake?" I was desperate to see him again.

"He is." She smiled down at me. "You can go and see him if you like."

I placed the cup of tea down on the table, balancing the donut on top and left her to wake Johnny. I slowly opened his door, afraid he'd be sleeping again.

He was sitting up in bed with a few pillows behind him, propping him up. He looked broken but I was happy to see his sparkle was still in his eyes. It quickly disappeared when a dark look crossed his face.

"What the fuck happened?" He sounded angry.

"I ran into an old friend." I cringed at how quickly this conversation had come up. I'd known he'd have questions but I just didn't have the answers he would want.

"Charlie?" he asked. He sounded jealous and as much as I loved the thought of Sammy getting jealous over me, now wasn't the time for this.

I stood at the end of his bed, feeling awkward. How the fuck was I going to explain this?

"Did you fuck him?" he asked bluntly.

"No!" I shouted, defending myself. "You think I would fucking do that to you?!"

"I don't know!" he snapped back. "When the guy that changed your entire fucking world leaves you with another guy and then that guy shows up and beats the fucking shit out of you... It tends to make you think of shit like that." His eyes filled with unshed tears before he looked away.

I sighed, taking a few steps around the bed so that I was closer to him.

"Sammy." I reached for his hand, needing the reassurance of his skin against mine. My fingers had barely grazed the back of his hand before he pulled away out of my reach.

I tried not to show how much it hurt to see him pull away from me. The fact that he didn't even want me to touch him said more than any words could have.

"I, uh..." I cleared my throat, swallowing past the lump that was lodged in my throat. "I would never do that to you, Sammy."

He leaned his head back into the pillows, staring up at me. His eyes had softened a little but there was still a lot of hurt there. A lot of hurt and pain that I had to make up for.

"I know you wouldn't," he whispered. "I just need to..."

"Need to what?" I asked, dreading his reply.

"I need to know what happened." He sighed, looking past me to stare at the wall. "I need the truth, Benjamin."

"Charlie did this," I replied.

I needed to be truthful to him. Charlie had destroyed all of the progress that we had made over the last few weeks. It felt like I was losing Sammy and I wasn't ready for that. I wasn't ready to admit defeat. Not yet.

"Charlie was a friend of mine. He left town about a year ago when he stole my wallet and ransacked the shop. He took the savings we had from the safe and destroyed all of our equipment." I sighed. "We had to close shop for a few months while we had everything renewed."

He frowned, looking at me with sympathy. "And now?" he choked out after a few moments of silence.

"And now he's come back. He asked me for money and when I told him to go and fuck himself, he and his buddies kicked the crap out of me." I sighed, hating the look of worry on his face. "Your friends Logan and Bex found me and took me back to her apartment where they wrapped my ribs and cleaned my cuts." I gestured to my face where most of my bruises were.

His eyes trailed over my body as if he was mentally taking notes of where I had been hurt.

I hated that with every word I said, I could see the shutters coming down. He was rebuilding the wall brick by brick that I had worked so hard to get past over the last few weeks.

I was losing him and it was plain to see.

"Sammy..." I placed my hand on his shoulder, hoping to offer some comfort. "All that matters is how I feel about you."

Looking into his beautiful green eyes, there wasn't much that I could say to fix this. All that I could offer him was the complete truth.

"I'm in love with you," I whispered.

His eyes widened in shock, caught off guard by my honesty.

I had never said those words to another person. I never thought I would ever say those words to anyone and mean them wholeheartedly. With Sammy, though... Sammy had stolen my heart since the moment I saw him at the skate park. My heart had fallen before my mind could even catch up and now... I never wanted it back.

I wanted to be his and only his but more than that, I wanted him to be happy.

Even if that couldn't be with me, I needed him know how I felt.

He was all that mattered.

SIXTEEN

Sammy

Sitting in that hospital bed staring at him, I wanted nothing more than to take his hand in mine and let him know just what I felt—how he had consumed my thoughts day and night and say that it was all going to be okay, but I couldn't.

It wasn't okay. We were both wearing bruises as badges of honor for the actions of someone else. I had been used as a punching bag because others thought that it was disgusting to be what I was. I was struggling with that.

These last few weeks with him had been wonderful. He had been so caring and gentle. Anytime I'd had questions or struggled, he'd always been there for me—patient and strong.

Somewhere along the way, I suppose I had let myself fall into a bubble and had now come to the point where my bubble and reality had crashed.

"Sammy..." he said, whispering my name like a prayer. He placed his hand on my shoulder, trying to offer some comfort.

I tried ignoring it but whenever he touched me, sparks of electric coursed through me.

"All that matters is how I feel about you."

He stared into my eyes for a few moments. It felt like there was a huge chasm divide between us and I didn't know how to close it. I couldn't honestly say that I wanted to.

I wasn't sure about anything right now.

"I'm in love with you," he whispered.

His words took me completely off guard. His honesty shocked me. We had never spoken about us on an emotional level and now... Now he was saying things that were only confusing me more.

"I, uh..." I looked away, not knowing what to say back to him. "I..."

He shook his head and squeezed my shoulder. "I didn't say it for you to say it back," he admitted. "I just wanted you to know what I was feeling."

He stroked his hand down my arm until he was grasping my hand.

I allowed him to hold it for a few moments before my brain kicked in, overriding my heart. I untangled my hand from his and pulled it away.

His face fell at my actions and I hated myself for what I was about to do.

I was going to hurt him, push him away, but this was going to hurt me more.

"I need time," I whispered, voicing my internal thoughts.

"Time away from me?" he asked, staring into my eyes.

I hated the unshed tears that I saw reflecting back at me. I hated more that I was the one that was causing it. Every time I had struggled over the last few weeks, Benjamin had been there by my side to help me through it. He had never left me and now...

Now I was leaving him.

"Time from everything," I admitted, trying to be as honest as possible. "A week ago, I was a member of the team. My life has been turned upside down and I..." I sighed, not knowing how to explain. "I have no direction. I need to decide what I want."

"What you want?" he asked, repeating my words back to me.

I nodded. "Yes. I came to this college for the football opportunities and now... Now I'm not sure what to do. I need to make some decisions and decide if I'm on the path I should be on. If staying here is the right thing to do or..."

"You'd move schools?" he asked, a note of shock in his tone. "Even after all of this?"

"I don't know," I replied. "I don't know what I want anymore and I need to figure that out."

He nodded, staring down at his feet. "I understand, Sammy."

I frowned, hating how easily the lie fell from his lips. How could he understand when I didn't even understand it?!

"I just need some time to decide what I want to do." I tried to sound positive to try and take the sting out of what I was asking of him but it didn't work. There was nothing I could say to make it better. Not at the moment.

He nodded before he stepped closer to the bed.

I thought he was going to kiss me but he didn't even try. He smoothed his hand through the top of my hair before he pressed a kiss to the top of my head. He left his lips there for a few moments longer than necessary.

"Take care of yourself," he whispered before he stepped away and left the room.

I stared after him, hating the way he had just

walked out—hating the way he had just left without saying a word. I was expecting him to shout at me or at least argue with me but... he just left.

I turned away from the door, cringing at the pain in my ribs. I closed my eyes before letting myself break, allowing the emotions out and feeling the crack that splintered through my heart.

The hospital discharged me later that afternoon with strict instructions from the doctors that I remained in the house on bed rest to give my ribs chance to heal. Tillie and Johnny took me home and made sure I stayed in bed.

I spent the next few days resting and catching up on my sleep before Johnny walked into my room. He looked nervous. "How are you feeling?" he asked, standing in my doorway.

I shrugged, feeling like crap. Things hadn't been right since Benjamin left. It had felt like he'd taken a chunk of me with him and I didn't know how to move past it.

I didn't know how to move past him.

"I'm okay," I answered. "Just sore."

He nodded before he took a few steps further in. "Can we talk?"

"Sure." I nodded my head and raised the remote, muting the television. "What do you want to talk about?"

He took a seat on the chair next to the bed that Tillie had moved there from her room. She had been coming in here to hang out with me in the evenings and apparently, she needed somewhere super comfy to sketch.

He took a deep breath before he turned to look at me. He had a troubled expression on his face. It was strange to see him look like that as Johnny always looked so chilled and relaxed.

"So, uh, Benjamin kind of left the hospital quickly..." He cocked an eyebrow at me.

"Uh..." *Fuck, he wanted to talk about this now?* "Yeah, I guess."

"You know that you can talk to me about anything," he said. He stared into my eyes before he continued. "You could have come to me." His voice broke on the sentence and I hated that my actions had hurt him.

It was never something that I wanted to do.

"I know but..." I looked at the doorway, shrugging my shoulders. "How the hell would I have started that conversation?" He opened his mouth to say something but I quickly continued before he could. "I didn't even know what I was so how was I supposed to talk about it with someone else?"

He continued staring at me, not saying a word.

"Am I that obvious?" I asked. I was worried that everyone else knew. Was I that obvious? Did Logan know?

"No, it's not obvious." He leaned back in the chair, rolling his eyes at me. "I mean, the insults all over the walls in the changing rooms were pointed and obvious but..." He looked back at me, the direction of the conversation swiftly changing. "This isn't about everyone else, Sammy. This is about you." He leaned forward, bracing his elbows on his knees. "What is it that you want?"

"I don't know..." I whispered. "Six months ago, my life was perfect. I knew who I was, where I was going and what I wanted. Now..."

"Now what?" he asked.

"Now I don't even know where I am." I shrugged my shoulders, feeling defeated. "Where do I go from here? What am I supposed to do?"

"Are we talking about school or Benjamin?" he asked, sounding a little confused.

"Both, I guess."

I never expected it to be so honest and easy discussing this with Johnny. Somewhere along the line, I had gotten it into my head that he wouldn't listen, that he wouldn't understand. How wrong I was.

"I guess it depends on what you want to happen next. Playing sports is out of the question but you still have your grades." He shrugged his shoulders. "I mean, you're not stupid, Sammy. You're a smart boy. If you focus on your grades and improving them a little more, it doesn't mean that you're out of the game completely. It could open up other avenues for you..."

He sounded so positive about that. So positive that I was 90% sure that he had already thought about this himself.

"And Benjamin?" I asked.

He shrugged his shoulders before he stood up. "That depends on you."

I sighed, leaning back into the bed and watched him walk out of the room.

My mind ran over everything that he had said. Maybe if I did pick my grades up, it could open other doors for me. Doors that I hadn't really thought about before.

As the days moved by slowly, Logan popped back and forth to check in and give me the latest gossip around campus. By this point, he had to have been to the arena and seen the mess those assholes had left behind. I was waiting for him to treat me differently in some way or talk to me differently but he never did. It hadn't seemed to bother him.

"Anything you want to talk about?" I asked, unable to stand it any longer.

He shook his head, looking confused by my outburst. "Not really." He grabbed the Xbox controller and passed it to me before grabbing his own and turning the system on. He took a seat in Tillie's chair before looking at me out of the corner of his eye. "It doesn't really bother me if someone thinks you're gay, bro. It does bother me that you took a battering for the rumor mill being in full operation." He shrugged his shoulders, an honest expression on his face. "I can still kick your ass at this game," he said with a cheeky grin on his face.

He didn't know.

A few hours later he left, leaving me to hang out with Tillie. We had fallen into a pattern of bingeing on cookie dough ice-cream and watching Disney films when Johnny had to go to practice. Tillie enjoyed it more than I did but it never bothered me as much as it would have bothered Logan. Especially since I enjoyed hanging out with Tillie.

Tillie had gone into 'protective mama' mode and had been making sure I had rest and no visitors. That lasted all but a few days before the team slowly descended on the house. I was thankful that Johnny was there to field some of the questions.

"So, what happened?" Jeremy asked. He was a junior student and had been friends with Johnny since he started college.

"We're too fucking good, that's what." Everyone laughed at Johnny when he said that. "Another team obviously not liking how well we're doing and wanted to take it out on one of our team."

Logan had learned that the boys Charlie had been hanging out with were on the Wolves football team. They were usually champions. It made sense that they would be easily led by Charlie to kick the crap out of one of us.

I appreciated him only giving out half-truths.

"I'm sorry, man," Jeremy apologized, looking at me.

I waved him off, not wanting the extra added attention. I got out of the armchair, letting Logan help me out of the seat.

"I think I'm going to go on up," I said, pointing my thumb at the ceiling.

Logan walked up the stairs behind me, going slowly. They had all turned a little protective since my beating. Logan had this scary reputation on campus as the bad boy and he was to a certain point but he was also sensitive.

I lay down on the bed, cringing when the springs squeaked a little too loudly. I was surprised that there wasn't a Sammy shaped imprint on the bed already due to how much time I spent up here.

A few hours later, Tillie entered the room. "So, what do you want to watch?" Tillie asked, smiling at me.

"You can pick," I said, not having the heart to name an action movie.

Tillie was at her happiest when there was anything Disney on the television. She was going to be an amazing mum one day.

She came back with two films: Dumbo and Die Hard. Not a good mix.

I raised my eyebrows in surprise. She hated the Die Hard films.

"I thought we could do one of each." She shrugged her shoulders, a faint blush covering her cheeks as she made herself comfortable in the chair.

We watched the movie in comfortable silence before she spoke up.

"So..." She looked at me before looking back to the screen. "I haven't seen Benjamin around. I thought he would have come by to visit before now."

Fucking hell. She wanted to talk about him now?!

I shrugged my shoulders, avoiding her gaze and giving my full attention to Dumbo and the mouse getting drunk with the floating elephants.

"He's been busy." I tried giving simple and blunt answers to throw her off the scent.

She turned her head to look at me and gave me a no-nonsense look.

I groaned, hating this conversation before it had even started.

"I, uh..." I frowned, trying to think of the best way to put it. "We kind of ended it."

Her face fell at my words. "But why?"

"I told him I wasn't sure what I wanted." I shrugged my shoulders, feeling at a loss for what to say. "Everything happened at once Tillie and I just... I don't know. I panicked, I guess."

"Is that why he left the hospital in such a rush?" She stared at me, seeing past all my bullshit.

I nodded, feeling a crushing sensation in my chest.

It still hurt the way that he had left. It had felt so... final. Like a goodbye.

"I thought so," she whispered. She looked so sad.

"Why?" I asked. "What gave it away?"

"He reminded me of Johnny that day."

I was confused. Johnny and Benjamin were complete opposites.

"Do you remember the day that I came back to town? After I'd been to visit my father?"

I nodded my head, remembering that day all too clearly. Johnny had been a wreck without Tillie. She had left town without telling him and he had been like a zombie around the place.

"When I entered his room after that, he had been lying on his bed holding the football." Her eyes filled with unshed tears at the memory. "He had looked so broken. We both were." She wiped beneath her eye, blinking hard to force the tears away. "That's how Benjamin looked when he left the hospital."

I looked away from her, hating the anger and sorrow that moved through me.

She scooted closer and took my hand in hers. "He loves you, Sammy. Just as I love Johnny and would do anything for him, I believe Benjamin loves you just as much." She sighed before smoothing my hair back. "He would do anything for you."

"But what if... what if it's not what I want? Or if it's not right for me?"

That was my biggest worry. What if it was a mistake? I would be changing my entire life and my family's lives for something that may not be strong or lasting. It was not only my whole life it would affect. I didn't want this to change Johnny's life and career if it wasn't as real and pure as Tillie believed it to be.

"Only you can answer that, Sammy." She stroked her hand down the side of my face, looking deep into my eyes. "But if you love him as much as I love your brother, it's not a question of what's right or wrong." She smiled, looking proud and strong. "It's about what you feel. If you feel as loved as I do when Johnny touches me, I want you to fight for that and never let anyone take it from you."

SEVENTEEN

Benjamin

When you tell someone that you love them, in a perfect reality, they say it back. Those three words I have never said to another person, not even Lily. It's something I never thought I would ever say but when I said to them to Sammy, I knew it was true. I knew that I would never again feel for another person for what I felt for Sammy

When we were together, it was perfect. He was my perfect fit.

I honestly never expected him to say them back. Not yet. I just wanted him to know how I felt for him. I expected it to bring us closer on an emotional level; not tear us apart.

"I don't know what I want anymore and I need to figure that out."

He didn't know what he wanted. That was what hurt me. I didn't need an *I love you*, but hearing him say that he didn't know if he wanted me – or us – it killed me.

I nodded, staring down at his feet, unable to meet his eyes. "I understand, Sammy."

I didn't understand. I would never understand. You either wanted someone in your life or you didn't.

"I just need some time to decide what I want to do," he said.

It almost seemed like he was trying to placate me for now but it was too late. The words had already been spoken and there was no way to take them back.

It was like Pandora's box. It had been opened and now there was no way to get the secrets back inside. I loved him and he didn't love me. I wasn't enough.

I nodded signaling that I had heard him before I stepped closer to the bed.

I wanted nothing more than to kiss him, to bring his lips to mine and attempt to show him... make him remember the warmth and passion that was between us.

There was no point.

I smoothed my hand through the top of his hair

for the last time before I pressed a kiss to the top of his head. I left my lips there for a few moments longer than necessary, breathing in his scent.

What I was about to do was going to hurt me a lot more than him.

"Take care of yourself," I whispered before I stepped away and left the room.

I didn't look back, unable to. If I did, I would never have been able to walk away from him.

I walked through the waiting room, avoiding Tillie's gaze. I needed to get out of there as fast as possible. I wasn't in the mood to put a smile on my face and pretend everything was okay. It wasn't okay and it never would be.

I jumped in the first taxi outside and directed him to my home. There wasn't a lot of traffic out. For some, the day hadn't even begun. It was only 7 am when I arrived home.

Walking inside, I kicked my shoes off and headed for my bedroom. I laid down on my bed, groaning when I smelt Sammy's scent on my pillow. He was everywhere and over the last few weeks, he had become a big part of my life.

Being with him wasn't easy but when it was him and me—just the two of us—it was so easy. Like breathing.

I hugged the pillow closer feeling the cracks in my chest. Losing Sammy had changed me. I was not the same man that I was before him. He had changed me for what I had thought was the better but now I didn't know.

I had never been a believer in soulmates. You only lived once and there was no such thing as love. After being with Sammy though, I knew I was wrong.

So fucking wrong.

I spent the majority of the day just lying on the covers, inhaling Sammy's scent. Lily had come by a few times but I just ignored her. I wasn't in the mood for her perky behaviour today. Right now, I just wanted to be left alone.

I rolled over, facing away from the door. Seconds later, a light tapping on my door sounded.

I frowned, wondering who it was. It couldn't be Lily: she didn't know how to tap lightly on a door. If she were at your door, you'd know about it.

Seconds later, I heard a key slide in the lock before footsteps moved through my lounge. The girl did not know how to get a hint. I didn't move. If she thought I was sleeping, chances were she would leave me alone to wallow in my misery.

She walked around the bed and looked down at me, tucking a stray curl back behind my ear.

I looked up at her and frowned when I saw how sad she looked.

"How is he?" she asked.

"He's okay." I shuffled backward, leaving her room to take a spot on the bed.

She laid down, lifting her black and red hair behind her so that it wasn't in the way.

"I went to the hospital," she whispered. "He went home this afternoon."

I nodded, hoping she had more details. He may not have wanted me there but I was still desperate for details.

"Why aren't you around there?" she asked. She sounded hesitant.

I stared at the heart-shaped locket hanging around her neck before meeting her eyes. "He doesn't want me."

Voicing it out loud seemed to make something snap inside. Up to now, I'd felt only sadness and numbness. Watching her eyes fill with tears, my own damn broke as a tear slid free.

"Sweetie, come here." She pulled my head into her

chest and I allowed her to. I let myself go, dropping the wall I had masterfully built to keep it all back.

"I thought... I thought he was diff..." I sobbed into her chest, hating how tight my chest was. It felt like I had a crushing sensation on my own chest. I sucked in a deep breath, feeling like my lungs were failing to expand.

"I know you did, Benji." She hugged me closer, trying to be strong. "So did I." She hiccupped on a sob and leaned her head down to rest on mine, holding me together as I allowed everything to break.

The days slowly passed and I had yet to return to reality. My job needed complete concentration and right now, but I just didn't have it. The boys were covering my shifts and Lily was flitting back and forth. I think she was afraid to leave me to sulk for too long on my own.

"Do you want anything to eat?" she asked, calling from the kitchen.

"No."

She was pissing me off and she had only been here a few minutes.

"You need to eat something," she called.

"I ate."

Lily was unique: you either loved her or hated her. Right now, I wasn't loving her overbearing protectiveness.

My attention was taken when there was a quiet knock on the door.

"I'll get it," she said, breezing in from the kitchen. She opened the door and her stance immediately changed to one with attitude.

"Is Benjamin here?" I recognized the voice immediately as belonging to Logan. What the hell was he doing here?

"No," she said. She closed the door to minimize the gap a little before she spoke again. "Who the hell are you?"

I took a few steps closer to Lily, wanting to know what he wanted.

"I'm Logan." His eyes flicked over her head and landed on me. "I need to talk to you."

I nodded and Lily slowly stepped back, opening the door further for him to come in.

"You look better," he said, eyeing my face.

"This is Lily," I said, introducing her.

She narrowed her eyes at him, showing her distaste.

He smirked at her in response, walking around her a little too close to her personal space before he took a seat on the sofa. He stretched his legs out and rested them on the edge of the coffee table.

In normal situations, I would have knocked his feet off it. He was grinning at Lily the whole time, trying to wind her up.

"Where the hell do you think you are?" she asked, screeching at him.

His eyes flicked to me before I gave him a pointed look.

He rolled his eyes, lowering his feet to the floor. "Where's Charlie?" he asked.

He looked serious for the first time since entering here and I knew that he was serious about this. Logan probably had it in his head to go looking for him and do what he did to Sammy.

"I don't know where he is," I said. It was an honest answer. I didn't know and I had no interest in finding out. Charlie had taken more than enough from me and I had no interest in losing anything else.

"Look, Ben," he snapped, getting to his feet. "My best friend is currently lying in a bed covered in bruises after getting a beating from your friend."

"Hey!" Lily yelled, walking up to him. She pointed her finger at his chest forcefully. "He is *nothing* to us. Charlie messed with us as well. So, before you start pointing fingers, you had better get your facts straight!"

I rolled my eyes at them. They were both as bad as each other. She was almost a foot shorter than him and there she was, trying to tell him off. It was comical.

"I don't know where he is," I interjected. "I want nothing to do with them. Either of them."

Logan turned to me, looking surprised by my outburst. "You don't mean that."

"Yes, I do." I crossed my arms, not in the mood for this. "Sammy made his feelings perfectly clear when he told me he didn't want me." My jaw tensed as I felt the hurt wash back over me. "Now I suggest you get out before I throw you out."

He looked down at Lily before looking back at me. His eyes widened in shock and I wanted to fucking kick myself. I had obviously just outed Sammy to his best friend.

"So, you two were...?" he waved his finger back and forth, putting it all together. He shook his head, looking frustrated. "And that's it?" he asked, shock evident in his tone. "After everything? You're just done with him?"

"Yes."

I was not fucking around.

He stormed past Lily and opened the front door,

grasping the edge of the door before he turned back to me. "This isn't over," he threatened before storming out and slamming it shut.

"Who the fuck was that?" Lily asked. She cocked her hip to the side, looking royally pissed off.

"He's Sammy's friend."

I walked into the kitchen, needing a drink. I took a bottle of water from the fridge, taking a sip before turning back around to face her.

"I don't like him." She scowled before continuing. "And?" She waved her hand in a rotating pattern for me to continue.

"He and his friend Bex found me on the street and dragged my ass back to her apartment. They cleaned my cuts up and wrapped my ribs before I hobbled back home."

"Well that was nice of him, I suppose." She shrugged her shoulders before she grabbed a bottle for herself. She stared up at me, fiddling with the lid for a few moments before she spoke up. "Did you mean what you said to him?"

"About what?" I asked. I knew which part she meant, but I needed her to be clear.

"About not wanting anything to do with Sammy?"

My jaw clenched when she said his name.

What did she want me to say? Admit that even the

sound of his name caused flutters to erupt in my stomach? Get angry at him and beg him to take me back? Break down into a crying mess again?

There was nothing I could say to justify what had happened between us. He had made his decision and that was it. Not much I could do, really.

"What do you want me to say, Lily?" I asked. "I loved him and I lost him."

She shook her head, looking sad. "No, I guess not."

Another knock sounded on the door and I hung my head, feeling frustrated. "If that's him again, I swear I am going to fucking punch him."

She giggled as I walked out of the kitchen. It was probably something she'd love to watch happen.

Opening the door, I was surprised to see who it was. Logan and Johnny stood there waiting for me to let them in.

"May we come in?" Johnny asked politely.

I left the door open and walked away, heading straight for the kitchen. If he had brought Johnny for back up, I was going to need something a lot fucking stronger than water.

"Who was it?" Lily asked. She was now sitting on the worktop nibbling on the end of a liquorice straw. Her eyes moved behind me before they widened in surprise.

She didn't know who he was but I'm sure she was figuring it out.

"Logan says he had a chat with you?" Johnny asked, cocking an eyebrow. He crossed his arms, causing the t-shirt to tighten around his biceps.

"Yes, and I'll tell you what I told him. I don't know where Charlie is and I don't want to know."

"Even after what he did to Sammy?" he asked.

He had to go there, didn't he?

"Yes," I ground out between clenched teeth. "Sammy and I no longer have anything to do with each other and I'd appreciate it if you'd just leave."

I nodded my head towards the door behind them, trying to get my point across.

Johnny looked at Logan as if he was waiting for him to say something. Logan only shrugged his shoulders in an 'I told you so' fashion.

"Sammy is hurt at the moment." Johnny turned his head back to me. "As he should be."

I stared back at him, refusing to back down.

"I know you're hurt as well," Johnny continued, softening his tone. "He just needs time, Benjamin."

I stared past him, refusing to acknowledge him.

"Benjamin!" Johnny snapped, forcing my attention back to him. "I am not leaving here without an address. That bastard beat my brother to a bloody pulp. You have two options. You either tell me where he is or you take me to him."

I stared at him, wondering how fucking serious he was. I could handle myself in a fight one on one but Johnny was bigger than I was. A lot fucking bigger.

"Now, what's it going to be?"

EIGHTEEN
Logan

I had never met anyone so fucking stubborn and arrogant. I thought Benjamin would have been just as angry as the rest of us. It was his fucking fault that all this shit had happened in the first place. He should have told Sammy that there was trouble coming; instead, he allowed him to walk around blind.

Walking out of his complex, I rolled my shoulders. I was tense as fuck since giving up football and swapping my credits over. Playing the game usually helped in relieving my stored up frustration. Since seeing Sammy in the hospital, I was itching to release my anger on the fucker that had put him in the bed.

Benjamin's voice echoed in my head as I walked back to the house where Johnny was waiting for me.

Sammy made his feelings perfectly clear when he told me he didn't want me.

The way he said it made it sound like there was more there than just friendship. I shook my head, thinking it over. Sammy wasn't gay. Was he?

Shouldn't I know if he was gay? There should be signs, right? Did I miss them?

Sammy and I had been friends ever since we were in kindergarten. We'd become inseparable since meeting. I could read him like a book and I knew when he lied to me. Had I become that much of a shit friend that I didn't even see that my best friend and brother was struggling?

I walked inside and saw Tillie coming down the stairs. She put her finger against her lips to indicate that Sammy was sleeping. I nodded and moved towards the kitchen where Johnny was waiting.

Johnny looked past me and frowned when he saw only Tillie. "Where is he?"

I shook my head. "He refuses to help."

Johnny stared at me for a few seconds before he shook his head and walked past me.

"Maybe you should leave it," Tillie said. "This family has been through enough, Johnny."

He froze his movements, his eyes moving to the

stairs before coming back to her. "He was hospitalized, Tillie. What do I do if it happens again?"

She sighed, looking down at the floor. She had no answer for him. There was nothing she could say.

He walked towards her and tilted her face up by placing his finger beneath her chin.

"It will be okay, baby girl." He gave her a quick kiss on her lips. "It's just going to be a friendly chat."

She stared up at him for a few minutes before she nodded. They both began walking towards the door before I stopped them.

"Hold up!" They both turned to look at me. "Are Sammy and Benjamin...?"

I left the question open, waving my fingers back and forth, needing someone to fill in the blanks.

They both looked at each other awkwardly. Tillie's cheeks tinged a pretty pink before they looked back to me, coming to a silent agreement.

"Yes," Johnny replied.

Yes? Seriously? That was all he was going to say? One fucking word?

Tillie rolled her eyes before chiming in. "It would appear they've broken up." She looked so sad.

"Fucking hell," I muttered. "Is there anything else I'm missing?"

I meant it as a joke but it's always best to ask.

Johnny shook his head and bent to kiss Tillie on her cheek. Seconds later, we were making our way to Benjamin's for some better results than last time. Hopefully...

Johnny knocked on the door before turning to me. "Let me handle this."

I nodded, taking a step back. I was determined to keep my mouth shut.

The door opened and Benjamin filled the doorway. He looked surprised when he saw who I had brought.

"May we come in?" Johnny asked politely.

Benjamin turned around and left the door open. He walked away and headed straight for the kitchen.

I looked around the lounge, looking for that little spitfire of his. She had a mouth on her; one I wouldn't mind using if the opportunity came up.

"Who was it?" Lily asked. Her voice came from the kitchen and I grinned, happy that I would get to see her in action again. She was sat on the worktop nibbling on the end of a liquorice straw looking at us with a look of surprise on her features.

I grinned, giving her a wink before her eyes narrowed into slits. I'd really pissed this one off and I couldn't wait to do it again. My eyes trailed down over her chest until they landed on her legs. Fuck me, I wouldn't mind having those wrapped around me as I fucked her on those worktops.

"Logan says he had a chat with you?" Johnny asked, looking at Benjamin. He crossed his arms and glared at him.

"Yes, and I'll tell you what I told him. I don't know where Charlie is and I don't want to know," Benjamin said, defending himself.

"Even after what he did to Sammy?" Johnny asked, shock evident in his tone.

He stared at Johnny for a few moments before he replied.

"Yes," he ground out between clenched teeth. "Sammy and I no longer have anything to do with each other and I'd appreciate it if you'd just leave." He nodded his head towards the door behind us.

He tried to mask it but you could hear the hurt in his tone.

Johnny looked down at me. His expression was pissed. It wasn't going to take much tonight for Johnny to snap.

I shrugged my shoulders in an 'I told you so' fashion, not pleased that we were going down this road again.

"Sammy is hurt at the moment," Johnny said, trying to reason. "As he should be."

Benjamin glared at Johnny, looking just as pissed off as Johnny seemed.

"I know you're hurt as well," Johnny said, trying a different angle by softening his tone. "He just needs time, Benjamin."

Benjamin stared past us.

I cringed as I felt the tension in the room begin to gradually rise.

"Benjamin!" Johnny snapped. "I am not leaving here without an address. That bastard beat my brother to a bloody pulp. You have two options. You either tell me where he is or you take me to him."

I cringed, wondering how long it was going to be before one of them snapped. It wouldn't take much.

"Now, what's it going to be?" Johnny asked in a threatening tone.

I hated watching Johnny lay the law down with Benjamin. I knew people thought I was an asshole and today was definitely one of those days. When you fucked with my family, you fucked with me.

I first met Sammy when we were in kindergarten. Since that day, we had been nothing but trouble for our mothers. Where one followed, the other was usually never too far behind.

When my mother died, I remembered being picked up from school. They took me to Sammy's home where his mother was. She took care of me as though I were one of her own. When I was put into the system, there was always a meal waiting for me at Sammy's whenever my own guardians forgot about me or couldn't be bothered.

It always meant the world to me that this family never forgot me.

I looked back at Benjamin, seeing the indecision written on his face. There was something else I couldn't fully grasp. I turned to Lily and saw the sadness that was on her face as she looked at Benjamin.

"Do you love him?" I asked, looking at Benjamin.

Benjamin's head spun towards at me. He still looked indecisive but I could also see hurt there.

"Do you love him?" I asked again, repeating my words.

I needed to know if he did. If he did, he was a bigger part of this than I had realized.

"Sammy needs you," Johnny said. "Sammy gets scared. He doesn't think things over like a regular person would." He shook his head, looking resigned. "Ever since high school, Sammy reacts first before thinking. If you feel for him like I think you do, you'll help us."

A moment of silence passed before I spoke up, hoping to reach him.

"Help us protect Sammy. If Charlie does it again and it's worse..." I shrugged my shoulders. "Johnny can shut Charlie down now before it gets out of hand. Before anyone else gets hurt again."

Benjamin flicked his gaze between Johnny and I before he turned his gaze back on Johnny.

"He'll be at Mason's bar," he said. He looked and sounded defeated. "It's across town by the town hall."

Johnny nodded. "I know where it is."

"I'll come with you," Benjamin continued.

Johnny stared at him for a few moments before he nodded his head. "Okay. But Charlie is mine. I want to see how he handles it when he's up against someone his own size."

Benjamin stared at him silently before nodding. "Let me go and change and I'll be with you."

Johnny nodded and followed after him. "I'll go and call Chunk."

I nodded, waiting for them both to clear the room before I walked over to Lily.

She grew tense as I approached her.

I leaned back against the worktop and stared at her, letting my eyes trail down her body and over those luscious legs in the 'fuck me' heels she was wearing.

"So, darling. I think you and I got off to a wrong start earlier."

She cocked a sexy eyebrow at me before she smiled sweetly. "You mean you're not usually a conceited asshole?" She crossed her legs and her skirt slowly rose up.

Fuck, she would be a handful.

I pushed off from the worktop and took a few steps closer until only a few inches separated us.

"I'll be whatever you need me to be, darling." Fuck, she smelled good. Like strawberries and cream.

She slid to the end of the worktop and lowered her feet to the floor. Her delectable little body was right in front of me and I wanted nothing more than for her to wrap her legs around me.

She leaned up on her tiptoes and placed her hands on my chest. "You wouldn't be able to handle me, Logan," she whispered in my ear.

She slid her body from in front of me, her sexy hips swinging from side to side as she walked away.

Fuck me! I adjusted myself and followed her. Lily was a fucking tease.

"I'm going now, Benjamin," she called as she walked towards the main door.

Benjamin nodded and followed her to the door. "Be safe."

She leaned up and gave him a kiss on the cheek. "You too. Call me when you're home."

He opened the door and closed it after her before he took a seat on the sofa. We waited patiently while Johnny finished up his phone call.

"Chunk is going to meet us there," he said, sliding his phone into his pocket.

"He'll have his boys with him," Benjamin said, getting to his feet.

He meant it as a warning but it did fuck all to worry Johnny.

"I hope he fucking does."

Johnny may have promised Tillie that this would be a friendly chat, but I knew better. Johnny was out for revenge and he wasn't going to stop until he got it.

We left the apartment and stood outside, waiting for Benjamin to unlock the car.

"You do know that Tillie is going to go fucking mental if you come home with bruises, right?" I asked Johnny.

He rolled his eyes and nodded. "I'm going to blame you." He chuckled before he got in the passenger seat.

Fucking great, I muttered to myself and climbed into the back.

NINETEEN
Johnny

The journey to Mason's bar took a little over forty minutes. The drive was mostly quiet except for Logan asking constant questions.

How long to go? What did Benjamin do for a job? Did he like working at Wicked Ink? Was Lily single?

I rolled my eyes when that question flew out of his mouth. I wasn't sure if Benjamin wanted to hit him or laugh.

"She's a lesbian, man," Benjamin admitted as he pulled the car to a stop outside the bar.

I tried not to laugh as I waited for Logan's reply.

"That shouldn't be a problem," he replied cockily.

I snicker before I opened the door, escaping from the very tense car. I spotted Chunk leaning up against the wall. His eyes landed on me before he and a few boys from the team walked over.

"How's it going, man?" Chunk gave me a quick hug before patting Logan on the back. "How do you want to do this?" he asked, directing his question to me.

"Nothing dramatic." I shook my head. "I just want to give him a friendly warning and leave."

Chunk cocked an eyebrow at me, not trusting my words.

"I'm serious." My fists clenched, thinking of the way he had allowed his goons to take turns punching Sammy. "If he wants to step outside, then that's another story." I smirked and walked towards the door. "You boys stay out here."

Logan looked at me like I had kicked his puppy.

"I'm serious. If we all go home with bruises, Tillie may throw me out." I chuckled at the thought of that happening.

I turned the door handle and left the boys outside with Benjamin. This wouldn't take long.

I walked inside and headed straight for the bar, ordering a coke and taking a seat on a stool. I paid the barman and waited. I looked straight ahead at the mirror and my eyes immediately landed on a few tables at the back of the room. They were all in green jerseys and laughing loudly.

I recognized the color immediately. *The Wolves.*

They were our competition and were *the* team to beat. This was about more than money and homophobia. These bastards wanted to fuck me off by taking my brother out of the running. They had obviously picked on the wrong Baker.

My eyes trailed over them, trying to figure out which fucker was Charlie. They all looked the same to me. Some had smaller body frames than others but they were all fucking cowards.

I froze when I heard footsteps approach and Logan and Benjamin took a seat on either side of me.

"What did I say?" I asked.

"I don't care," Logan replied, catching my gaze in the reflection. "We're a family."

"Where is he?" I asked, directing my question to Benjamin.

His gaze ran over the mirror in front of us before he shook his head. "He's not here."

"For fuck's sake!" I muttered, feeling pissed off.

How many places did I have to go to give an ass-kicking?

The door to the bar opened before an obnoxious laughter filtered through. Seconds later, some of our teammates followed into the bar from where they were waiting outside. They were glaring at the asshole with the too loud laugh and that's when I knew.

"That's him," Benjamin whispered.

I nodded my head and took another sip of my coke. I tried to ignore the anger and fury that was moving through me but I couldn't switch it off. I wanted to fucking kill him.

He leaned his hands on the table and I waited as one of his boys whispered something to him. Seconds later, every one of them was staring in my direction.

Charlie straightened up and made his way over. He ignored Benjamin completely and tapped the back of my shoulder.

I turned in my seat and looked at him.

"I'm afraid you're not welcome here," he said with a sickening smile on his face.

I looked at Logan before shrugging and looking back to him. "We're not bothering anyone."

"You're bothering me." Four of his teammates got out of their seats and came to stand behind him. "I don't like gays in my bar." His eyes flicked to Benjamin and he looked at me with disgust.

"You don't like gays but you don't mind stealing from them?" I asked, my voice dripping with sarcasm.

"Or beating them up and leaving them in a vandalized part of school property?"

I tried keeping the anger from my tone but I wasn't successful. I wanted to rip his fucking head off —deliver back every single punch that he had blown down on Sammy.

His friends behind him snickered.

"Can't handle losing on the field, can we, boys?" I mocked.

Their snickering stopped instantly.

"How is little Sammy doing?" Charlie asked, dropping all pretense. His eyes flicked to Benjamin again before coming back to me. "Is he walking yet?"

Logan's foot twitched on the bar and I held my hand up immediately, stopping him from moving. He settled back in the stool, attempting to retain his anger.

They snickered again, watching me hold Logan back. I took a step down from the bar and smirked when the grin left Charlie's face. I was a good few inches taller than he was and he and I both knew he was fucked if he was going to go up against me.

"Sammy is my brother," I said, trying to keep a grasp on my anger. I looked at the boys behind him before looking back to Charlie. "If any of you fuckers touch him again, it'll be the last thing you do."

I maintained eye contact with Charlie, needing to get my message across.

A few moments later, he nodded his head and took a step back. "That shouldn't be a problem."

Logan fidgeted where he was sitting and I knew he was expecting more. Truth be told, so was I.

"Let's go," I said, turning to Logan. He was half out of his seat before it all went to fucking hell.

"Yes, go. And take this gay fucker with you," Charlie said, indicating Benjamin.

I froze, my anger rising.

Charlie turned and started walking away. Before he could get too far, I grabbed his shoulder and spun him around.

"Johnny, no!" Benjamin yelled.

It was too late. These fuckers were never going to stop.

I slammed my fist into Charlie's jaw and knocked him to the ground. Before I knew it, all of us were in the thick of it and this shit suddenly went from bad to fucking worse. Except for Chunk. Chunk had about three of them on him. It didn't last long before Benjamin was over, evening the fight out a little.

I slammed my fist down on Charlie before he knocked me backward, getting a lucky punch in the jaw. His body landed on mine, pinning me to the floor while he began pounding his fists down on me.

I raised my fist and knocked him off me, loving the way his body toppled off mine.

Before I could go after him again, the sound of a gunshot echoed through the room. I quickly got to my feet and looked at the bar. The barman was stood behind there, looking really pissed off.

"That's enough!" he yelled. "You boys." He pointed at me and Logan. "Out!"

"Just clearing up a disagreement." I turned to Charlie and glared at him, narrowing my eyes. "We clear?"

He stared at me for a few minutes before he nodded his head. "I'll see you around Baker!"

It was said as a threat but I took it as a fucking promise.

"Let's go." I nodded my head to the door indicating for every one of my boys to go first. "Don't touch Sammy again," I said, walking away.

Charlie narrowed his eyes at me and watched me go.

I knew he had no interest in touching Sammy again. I had caught his attention and I could see it had now shifted to me. I wouldn't be so easy to knock around as Sammy was, though.

I walked outside and cringed when I saw the rest of the team. They all handled themselves perfectly but I could see there would be definite bruises tomorrow.

"Thanks for coming, man," I said, tapping fists with Chunk.

"Anything for Sammy, man." He grinned at me before he walked away, going to his vehicle.

I climbed into Benjamin's car, groaning at the pounding in my head. I flipped the visor down and took a quick look in the mirror. Apart from a bloody nose and a bruising jaw, it wasn't too bad.

The drive was mostly silent on the way home before Benjamin decided to break the silence.

"He's going to play dirty."

I chuckled, rolling my eyes. "Thanks for stating the obvious."

He laughed, finding my reply funny. The car came to a stop before he looked over at me. "Just be careful, okay?" He cocked an eyebrow at me, waiting for a reply.

"Sure." I nodded my head and took a few steps away from the car with Logan following me. "Maybe we'll see you around soon." I gave him a quick salute and began walking our way home.

Logan looked up at me and I frowned when I realized he was limping a little.

"Fucker stomped on my ankle." He rolled his eyes before he continued. "Fucking pussies."

I slowed my pace to make it easier for him.

"Tillie is going to go fucking mental," he said, grinning.

I laughed, tossing my head back, knowing how fucking correct that statement was.

TWENTY
Sammy

Walking downstairs, I went slowly, holding on to the banister the whole way. I still wasn't great on my feet but the pain in my ribs had eased. I could hear voices but couldn't make out what they were saying until I got to the bottom of the stairs.

Tillie, Johnny and Logan were in the kitchen and it looked like they were having a disagreement.

"You were supposed to keep him out of trouble!" she said, spinning to look at Logan.

"Me?" He was trying not to laugh. "Have you seen the size of him?" He waved his hand towards Johnny. "It'd be like a smurf holding back a fucking giant."

I snickered, imagining it. "Did you just call yourself a smurf?"

All three of them turned to look at me before Tillie was moving forward. "What are you doing out of bed?" She took my arm and began steering me back to the sofa.

"I'm okay, Tillie." I remained standing, needing to stretch my legs. This lying around routine was doing my head in. I gave her a gentle smile before looking back to the boys.

"What the hell happened?" I asked, shocked when I saw bruising covering Johnny's jaw.

Logan walked towards me and it looked like he was leaning most of his weight on his right side.

"We went and had a private chat with Charlie," Johnny said.

I narrowed my eyes at him. Why the fuck did I have to belong to such a meddlesome family.

"Johnny..." I started.

"Don't." He said it with such attitude that I immediately backed down. "Do you have any idea how it felt? To find you on that cold and wet floor and not know if you were going to even wake up?" He glared at me and I could see the hurt that he was feeling. "Enough shit has gone on lately. Charlie and I had a friendly chat and he won't be a problem any longer."

I nodded, letting it pass. I knew Johnny well

enough to know that when he was in this kind of mood it was best to leave it well enough alone.

"Benjamin was with us," Logan said, chiming in from his spot by the window.

I groaned, turning around and walking towards the sofa. Maybe I should have stayed in bed. "Is he okay?" I asked. I both dreaded and needed the answer.

How we'd left things had been plaguing me. I'd thought that by pushing him away and moving the focus to my grades and my future would have made things easier for me—that it would have made our situation less important but now...

I was so fucking wrong. He was still all that I thought about. All that I wanted.

There was a hole in my chest where he used to be and it wasn't healing. The bruises on my face had started to heal and my side felt a lot better but my chest... The ache was always there, as though a dull weight was wedged there.

"Yes, he's okay." Johnny nodded and took Tillie's hand in his, playing with the ring on her finger. "I was impressed with how well he handled himself." He grinned at me, showing that he was teasing.

"Why didn't you tell us?" Logan asked, directing his question to me. "You could have told one of us."

He sounded hurt that I hadn't chosen to confide in one of them.

I shrugged, not really knowing how to answer that question. "I don't think I really knew." I shrugged my shoulders, trying to be honest. "When I first met Benjamin, I didn't know that what I was feeling for him was an attraction."

Logan frowned but I quickly continued, trying to find the words to give them the answers they were looking for.

"I knew it was something but I just wasn't sure what it was."

Tillie walked over and took a seat next to me. She took my hand in hers and rested her head on my shoulder. One of the many reasons I loved Tillie was moments like this. She knew how to be there for people without needing to be asked. She was special that way.

"Over the weeks, we took some time to get to know each other and things slowly developed. I freaked out a few times but every time, Benjamin would always take the time to talk to me and... He really listened. I've never had that before."

Johnny turned his head to look at Tillie and they smiled at each other across the room. It was a private smile. A smile meant only for them.

They knew what I was talking about because they had that with each other.

"But you're not together anymore," Logan stated.

"No." I shook my head, feeling the knot in my chest tighten. "Lying in that hospital bed, I freaked out. Again." I rolled my eyes at myself, realizing how much of an idiot I had been. "I told him that I wasn't sure what I wanted and I... We parted ways, I guess."

"So, you fucked up, in other words," Logan commented. Blunt as ever.

I rolled my eyes, happy that Logan could at least see the humor in all of this.

"Yeah, I guess I did." I looked past him, resting my head on the back of the sofa. "And now I have to try to fix it."

"Just be honest with him," Tillie said, lifting her head from my shoulder. "That's how Johnny and I got past our problems.

I nodded, giving her a small smile. Before I could open my mouth to ask her more, Logan started talking again.

"When I fuck up, I usually send flowers." He paused to look at Johnny. "Do gay men get flowers?"

"Logan!" Tillie admonished, getting up from her spot on the sofa.

"What?" He had no clue what she was telling him off for. He was trying to help in his own way.

"I don't think flowers will fix this." I chuckled.

Whoever would end up with Logan had a hard job ahead of them.

"We're going to go over to Joy's," Tillie said. "Is there anything you need?"

I shook my head. "No, I'm good, thanks. I'm going to go back upstairs and do some of my essay."

They nodded and left the house, leaving me with Logan.

I got off the sofa and turned to look at my friend. "Are we cool?"

I was afraid to ask that question but it was a question that needed asking, none the less.

He rolled his eyes and walked towards me. He wrapped his arms around me and tapped me on the back.

"Of course we are, man." He pulled back before speaking again. "Just don't lie to me again, okay? I can't help if I don't know there's a problem."

I nodded before taking a seat back on the sofa. "Game of FIFA tonight?" I asked.

"Sure." He stared at me silently before he grabbed his keys. "See you later, man," he said, before he walked out the front door, heading to his afternoon class.

I sat there for a few moments, enjoying the peaceful silence.

Just be honest with him. Tillie's voice echoed in my head.

Benjamin had always been honest with me—up until Charlie walked back into town, at least. Any time I'd had a problem or I'd got scared, he'd always been there. He'd never failed me and now I had failed him.

Fuck this.

I grabbed my keys and scribbled a note for Tillie before I began making my way to Benjamin's. Chances were he may not be in but I couldn't just sit there and wait around obsessing over him any longer.

I pressed the buzzer for his apartment and waited. After the third press, I was beginning to think that he wasn't here. Before I could turn away, I grinned when I saw Lily walk towards me from the other side of the door.

She opened the door and wrapped her arms around me, squeezing me tightly. "I missed you," she whispered.

I laughed, pulling back. "I missed you, too." I looked past her at the stairs leading up to his floor before looking back at her. "How is he?"

She frowned, a look of sympathy crossing her face before she shook it off. "He's better today." She narrowed her eyes at me in speculation. "Be good to him, Sammy. He's one of the decent ones."

"I know." I sighed a deep breath. "I messed up."

"We all do it." She gave me a cheeky wink before giving me a quick kiss on the cheek. "Now go and fix it." She held the door open for me and left me to it.

Lily was my angel.

I walked up the stairs slowly, trying to give myself some extra time to think it over. I still had no fucking clue what I was going to say to him.

What if he wouldn't answer the door? What if he was done with me? What if I had pushed him a step too far? What if he thought he was better off without me? What if he was?

No!

I shook my head, trying to chase all the negative thoughts away. People don't just say 'I love you' to people they are better off without. As far as I knew, Benjamin had never said those words to another person before.

It meant something. It meant everything.

I raised my hand to knock but before my fist could make contact, the door was pulled open. I gasped, taking a step back. Benjamin was standing there with only one arm slid into his leather jacket.

His eyes widened in surprise when he saw me

before he frowned. "What are you doing here?" he asked. He looked and sounded confused at the sight of me stood in his doorway.

"I came to see you," I whispered. I wanted to kick myself. He looked so pale and I could see that he had lost a little weight. "Can we talk?" I asked.

He nodded, taking a step back. I walked in and closed the door, smiling at him.

He shed his coat and hung it up on the hook by the door. "Do you want a drink?"

I nodded and followed him into the kitchen. "How has work been?" I asked, trying to bring a bit of normality into this tenseness.

"I haven't been." He grabbed two bottles of beer from the fridge before uncapping them and sliding one across the counter to me. "The boys have been covering my shifts."

"Why?" I was confused. Had they had a falling out?

"Because my concentration wasn't at 100%." He took a swig of his drink and looked away, avoiding my gaze.

The silence stretched between us and I knew what he wasn't saying. It was because of me. He wasn't at work because of me.

"I'm sorry," I whispered. I looked down and began picking at the label on my bottle. "I didn't mean..."

The silence hung between us. I could feel his gaze on me.

"Didn't mean what?" he asked.

"To hurt you," I whispered, looking up at him. "I never wanted to hurt you. I just got scared and I..." I sighed deeply. "I just wanted to push you away, I guess."

His beautiful green eyes burned into mine, capturing me. "And now what?" he asked. "Now what do you want?"

"You," I whispered. "I just want you."

I jumped in shock as he slammed his bottle down on the counter and walked over to me. I wasn't sure if he was angry at me or turned on. I was hoping for the latter but I was also expecting a right hook. Especially after all the shit I had put him through.

I placed my bottle down on the counter and turned my body towards him.

His hands grasped hold of my face and he pushed me back against the counter and placed his lips on mine, sucking on my bottom lip before pulling back. "It took you long enough," he whispered before he pressed his lips back against mine.

I gasped and parted my lips, allowing his tongue

entry. I groaned as our tongues pressed against each other's. He wrapped his arms around my waist, pulling my body closer to his. I slid my arms up around his neck before threading my fingers into the curls at the back of his hair.

"I'm sorry I took so long," I whispered, pulling back.

He leaned his forehead against mine and stared into my eyes. "I missed you," he whispered.

I smiled, loving those words. "I missed you too."

"So." He gulped, his Adam's apple bobbing up and down. "What happens now?" He looked so nervous.

"Now?" I tucked a stray curl back behind his ear. "Now, you get to meet my crazy world."

He chuckled and pressed his lips back to mine before leading me back to the lounge where we stayed for the rest of the afternoon, talking about everything: Charlie, football, classes... the future.

My future was right here... with him. For as long as he'd want me.

TWENTY-ONE

Benjamin

I wasn't a nervous person. Never had been. Even when I was a kid, I was always calm and relaxed. However, standing outside Joy's home, I was man enough to admit that I was freaking out.

Joy was the first person that Sammy had ever spoken to about his feelings for me. It was due to her wisdom and advice that I had everything with Sammy that I have now. She'd lent him a friendly ear when he needed one the most—when he had no one else. For that, I owed her everything.

I sighed, rolling my shoulders to try and ease some of the tension. I turned when I heard footsteps approach. I knew who it would be before he spoke.

"You're not nervous, are you?" Sammy asked. He

had a teasing grin on his face and it made me want to kiss it off.

"Why would I be nervous?" I asked, trying to act cool and calm.

"Because you've been standing out here for the last twenty minutes and you haven't even come in." He pointed his thumb toward the door behind him.

Fucking busted. "I was early and I didn't want to..."

He cocked an eyebrow at me with a disbelieving expression on his face. He held his hand out for mine and I immediately took it.

"She doesn't bite," he teased, leading me forward.

"What if she doesn't like me?" I asked, muttering under my breath.

"Impossible." He shook his head, tightening his grip on my hand. "Joy loves everybody."

I rolled my eyes at him, not believing him. If this lady didn't like me, I would be well and truly fucked.

Sammy opened the door and pulled me inside. It made me proud that he didn't even try and unclasp our hands. He stood with his head held high and looked at his family with me by his side.

I smiled at the gang that stood around the room before my eyes were instantly taken by Joy. She walked forwards and came straight towards us.

"Joy," Sammy said, unclasping his hand from mine and wrapping his arm around her shoulders. "This is Benjamin."

I smiled down at her and held my hand out for her to shake. "It's a pleasure to meet you."

She smiled up at Sammy and they both chuckled. She stepped forward out of his hold and shook her head at me. "We hug in this family, sweetie."

I was surprised as hell when she pulled me down into a tight hug. I looked over at Sammy and smiled when I saw how happy he looked. This woman meant the world to him and it was then that I realized I would do anything for her—just for that reason.

Just for how much Sammy adored her.

She pulled back and smiled up at me. "I'm so glad you could join us for dinner, Benjamin."

Seconds later, I was being shown where to sit at her table. Looking around, I saw that this was a very special place to be. This was a family not bound by blood; they were bonded by something so much more.

Love and loyalty.

It was the two secret ingredients of any family and this one had it in buckets.

"You okay?" Sammy asked, turning to me. "You seem to be a little zoned out."

I shook my head and looked around the table before looking back at him. "It's perfect."

He smiled, leaning over and pressing a quick kiss to the corner of my mouth before pulling back.

The rest of dinner was followed by conversation, wine and the most gorgeous fudge cake I had ever tasted. I would have licked my plate if I'd been at home.

"Well, thank you for an amazing dinner once again," Sammy said, thanking Joy.

"Yes, it was lovely," I chimed in. "Thank you for having me."

Everyone stood and Sammy turned to Joy and gave her a small hug.

We made our way to her doorway where hugs were once again exchanged. It didn't take a genius to figure out that these kids were her heart.

"You boys look after each other," she said, waving us off at the door.

We gave her a small wave before we disappeared up the street towards my apartment.

"So, what did you think of Joy?" Sammy asked, taking my hand in his.

"Her fudge cake is to die for." I grinned, loving the smile that stretched across his face.

Sammy had many smiles: cheeky, wicked, excited,

bashful... The one he was using right now was my favorite. It was one that I didn't see often but one that I knew meant more than the others.

This was his happy smile. I was determined to see more of it than I had in the past.

"She's an amazing cook," he agreed, nodding his head. "And she loved you."

I grinned, loving to hear that I got the thumbs up. Especially from her.

Arriving back at the apartment, I turned to take his coat from him and groaned when I realized how fuckable Sammy looked in a shirt and tie. He looked good in anything but when he was dressed formally, I just wanted to lock him in my room.

I took a step towards him and took his tie in my hand. I pulled him closer and pressed my lips to his.

"You look very good in a shirt," I whispered, nibbling on his bottom lip

He grinned, pulling back. "I look even better out of it."

I gasped, pulling his lips back to mine. I wouldn't last long with Sammy if he was going to start talking to me like that. It made me think of what he'd be like to fuck and that was something I really shouldn't be thinking about.

Especially when I was alone with him.

He slid his arms up over my shoulders and began pushing me backward in the direction of the sofa.

Since Sammy had come out to his family, he had become a lot more confident when it came to touching me. Before he was always so hesitant and now... Now he touched me with more passion. When we kissed, he would pull me against him as though he never wanted to let me go. The feeling was more than mutual.

We toppled on to the couch with Sammy's body on top of mine. He wasted no time and rocked his hips against mine before he dipped his head and pressed open-mouthed kisses against the column of my neck.

I groaned, loving the feel of them on my skin. I grasped the back of his head and threaded my fingers through the thick strands of his hair, wanting him closer.

He chuckled against my skin before he brought his mouth back to mine.

I reached up and grabbed the knot of his tie and began undoing it. I was waiting for his body to go tense—it occasionally happened when I unknowingly pushed him too far—but it didn't. He pushed his body firmer against mine and his hands became eager as he reached down and pulled the shirt out from beneath my belt.

His fingers grazed over my stomach above my belt

and I knew he could feel how hard I was for him. If he kept going, he'd be doing a lot more than just feeling me through my trousers.

I loosened his tie enough and quickly yanked it over his head.

He chuckled at my eagerness and his fingers slowly moved to my belt. Before he could even begin to unbuckle me, we were interrupted by a loud bang on the door. He moved his head to look at the door but there was no fucking way I was stopping this.

"Ignore it," I said, turning his head back to me and roughly brought his lips back to mine. He thrust his tongue into my mouth as I reached up and began sliding the top buttons on his shirt undone.

Bang. Bang. Bang.

I groaned, leaning my head back into the cushion. "This is not fucking happening," I ground out before gently moving Sammy aside and making my way to the door.

I swung the door open, determined to tell whoever it was to fuck off when I froze at the sight that stood in front of me.

Lily.

She stood in the hallway, wearing her black dress with white streaks on it and a pair of black flats. She had a day off today and was supposed to be spending it with Trixie. Now, she was on my doorstep with mascara streaks smudged on her face. She had been crying and she looked a complete mess.

I didn't recognize this Lily. This Lily was a stranger.

"What's wrong?" I asked. My Lily never cried. She was a fighter. Even when the shop was ransacked, not once did she cry. It broke her heart but not once did I see her cry.

"I went home," she said, a sob breaking free as she walked in.

"Lily!" Sammy said, shock in his tone.

I wasn't sure if it was shock to see her here or shock that she was a sobbing mess.

"What happened?" He held his hands out to her, offering her comfort.

I was shocked as hell when she went straight to him. He wrapped his arms tightly around her. He lowered himself to the sofa and pulled her down with him, letting her cuddle into him by laying her head on his chest.

"What happened, sweetheart?" I asked, rubbing the back of her shoulder.

She was silent for several moments, staring at the wall while Sammy stroked the back of her head. Her eyes closed as another tear slipped free before she spoke. "I saw Trixie with another girl." She looked broken.

Sammy looked over her head at me and I could see that he had no clue what to say. What do you say in situations like that?

"Maybe they were just friends?" I asked, trying to find a reasonable solution. Lily was a stunning girl... Trixie would have to be fucking crazy to do that to her.

"We were supposed to have dinner tonight," she whispered. She reached up and wiped the wetness from her cheek before continuing. "We've been distant with each other lately and I thought it'd be a nice excuse for us to spend some quality time together. Lately, we only see each other in the evenings after work."

I nodded my head, empathetically. "That sounds like a good idea."

She nodded her head and took a deep breath. "This afternoon she called to say she couldn't make it because she had to work a few hours extra because a colleague had called in sick." She shrugged her shoulders. "I told her it was fine and that I would see her at home tonight."

I nodded, dreading the next part of this story.

"Then what?" Sammy asked after a few moments of silence. He tightened his arms around her, almost as though he was giving her extra comfort for this next part.

"Tyler and Darren told me that I should join them for drinks. They were going out with some friends after work and said I should tag along." Another tear. "We had been at Club 101 for about an hour before I stood up, planning to leave. I wanted to be there when Trixie got home. I was going to run her a bath and make some dinner for her."

She hiccupped a sob and it broke my heart.

"I waved over at Tyler and pointed over my shoulder indicating that I was going to leave." She sucked in a deep, shaky breath and her hand tightened on Sammy's shirt. "Sh-she was there, dancing with another girl."

I had never hit a woman before but if Trixie was here right now...

"She kissed her and I... I couldn't stay there." She shook her head and her shoulders drooped. She looked like she had no more fight left in her. "I ran and I... I came straight here."

She sobbed hard, pushing her face into Sammy's chest. Sammy shifted her to the side and moved her so that she was sitting across his lap. He cuddled her close and rocked her slowly.

Watching them together, I knew how lucky I was. I

had built an amazing family around me and by finding Sammy, I had found everything I had ever wanted or needed. Even when I didn't believe in the kind of love that I had seen Tillie and Johnny share, you couldn't argue that it wasn't real.

Love was real and I had somehow been lucky enough to find it and keep it.

Several moments later, her sobs had slowly quieted down. Sammy still held her close and comforted her by stroking her hair back. Her body had slumped under his relaxing touch and she looked completely exhausted.

Exhausted and sadly broken.

A quiet knock sounded on the door and I knew who it would be before I even opened it.

Tyler.

"Is Lily here? She's not at home or the shop." He had Darren with him and they both looked frantic.

I nodded and held the door open for them and waved my hand to where Sammy sat with a cuddled up Lily.

Tyler sighed. "Trixie has really fucked this one up," he muttered before he walked towards her. "Is she sleeping?" he asked, directing his question to Sammy.

He shook his head before answering. "No, she's just tired."

He nodded before he slid his hands beneath her. She wrapped her arms around Tyler's shoulders and he lifted her up.

"Let's go home, baby sis," he said, tightening his grip on her. Darren followed him and left the apartment, leaving Sammy and me alone.

"Poor Lily," Sammy whispered.

My eyes moved down to his chest and I chuckled when I saw the front of his shirt. He was soaked from Lily's crying.

"Do you think she'll forgive her?" he asked.

I shook my head and walked over, taking a seat next to him. "No way. You get one shot with Lily. If you fuck it up, that's it."

His eyebrows rose in surprise. "But she's too sweet to be that harsh."

I smiled. "I guess it depends on what you do to her. If you steal the last chocolate sprinkle donut, she may move past it."

We both chuckled at the idea of that. If you valued your life, it was rule number one in the shop to never touch the chocolate sprinkled donuts. The girl was obsessed with anything chocolate.

"But what Trixie has done?" I shook my head sadly. "Could you forgive me if I did that to you?"

I stared at him, waiting for him to answer. His face

dropped and I knew that he understood. "I don't think so," he whispered. "You don't do that to someone you love."

I raised my arm, offering him a spot. He laid his head against my shoulder and cuddled himself closer. I tried not to read too much into his words.

It wasn't an 'I love you', but it was closer to one than I'd ever been before.

TWENTY-TWO
Sammy

It had been several weeks since Lily's psychotic breakdown.

Her words, not mine.

Since then, she'd gone around and boxed up all her items and moved in with Tyler. Every time I had seen her since, she had insisted that she was fine and always seemed to have an extra bounce in her step.

She seemed okay but we all still worried about her. You didn't get over a break-up that easily. When I thought back to when Benjamin and I parted ways at the hospital, I still got angry over it.

In Lily's words; it wasn't meant to be and fate had other plans for her.

Maybe that was how she was. Maybe she just reacted differently to the rest of us.

I entered the shop, sneaking in and being careful not to be too loud. I wanted to do something special for Benjamin that night and Lily was helping me out by lending me a copy of the key to his apartment. Tyler kept a copy for safekeeping and I was stealing it tonight.

"Do you have it?" I asked, keeping my voice low.

"Hey, Lily!" Benjamin called from his room. It was followed by footsteps coming in this direction.

I looked at Lily panicked before she theatrically waved me around the counter. I crouched down on my knees, hiding from Benjamin.

"Has that vibrant red ink come in yet? One of our regulars wants some fresh ink but it has to be in that color," he said.

I looked up and saw his fingers grab on to the top partition of the counter.

She cocked her hip and stared at him, looking pissed off. "Don't I usually tell you if we've had a delivery?" She raised her eyebrows, trying to intimidate him.

He sighed and walked away, going back to his station.

The second he disappeared, she shot out the other

side of the counter and raced to the door, holding it open for me and held the key out.

"You rock!" I gave her a quick kiss on the cheek and grabbed the key before running out, the sound of her giggles following behind me.

After a quick stop to the store, I arrived back at Benjamin's and got straight to work in the kitchen. Tillie had offered to help and make me a lasagne just in case I fucked this up but I turned her down. I wanted to do this on my own.

I did accept a freshly baked fudge cake, courtesy of Joy, though. Benjamin loved her cake and he had been round to Joy's a few times on his own to just hang out with her. They had really come to like each other and many times, I would pop round and be surprised to see him sitting at her table with a plate of cookies between them.

Benjamin got along with all my family, to be honest. He had become one of Logan's latest Xbox buddies, and when I was home, I would often hear Logan shouting into his headpiece at Benjamin. His language usually had Tillie tapping him on the head and telling him to lower his voice.

He didn't understand football but he was trying to learn the rules when Johnny and he would watch a game together. He had also tried to connect with

Tillie by sitting for her to learn her shadows more but it didn't go well. Apparently, he fidgeted too much.

I chuckled when I thought back to the little frown that Tillie wore as she tried to draw him. They were both artists in their own way and Benjamin had tried to convince Tillie to join Johnny when he came into the shop to have his piece done but she wasn't budging.

I grabbed the saucepans from the cupboard and got to work. I'd decided to make his favorite meal of spaghetti bolognaise and meatballs. Benjamin loved it but he never took the time to cook it as it often went to waste. Plus, he had been eating at my house a lot lately which was nice.

An hour later, I was standing at the stove, facing away from the doorway, when I felt a pair of strong arms wrap around my waist.

"What's this?" he asked, whispering in my ear. He rested his head on my shoulder and turned his mouth, pressing a kiss to the column of my neck.

"I wanted to do something special for you," I admitted, turning my head and getting a quick kiss.

He smiled before stepping away from me. "Well, it smells delicious in here..." His eyes moved past me to the white parcel on the side. "Is that fudge cake?" he asked, pointing at it. His voice had risen a few levels with enthusiasm.

"Maybe." I giggled at his reaction to the thought of Joy's fudge cake.

He chuckled and placed his wallet on the side before turning back to me. "Anything I can do to help?" He raised his eyebrows, waiting for my response.

"Sure." I nodded my head at the cutlery placed on the side. "Do you want to lay them out and I can then serve up?"

I had made two lots of spaghetti: one with meat and a vegetarian option for myself. I didn't try to force my vegetarian preferences on anyone else. I just preferred not to eat meat.

"You shouldn't have made two lots," he defended when I took my seat next to him. He placed his hand on my leg and rubbed. "I would have eaten whatever you were having."

He said it to comfort me and it was very sweet of him. I don't think he meant the rubbing to be taken sexually but that was all I could think about when his hands were on me.

In the past, I had never been a highly sexual person. I had been with more than a few girls but unlike Logan, I didn't have a high sexual appetite. Although over the last couple of weeks, every time that Benjamin touched me, all I could think about was being with him.

I had never done anything too adventurous with girls in the past. It had always been missionary: a quick fuck and we'd both be on our way. I had never been into relationships and neither had any of my fuck buddies.

With Benjamin, though, I was both scared and excited to be with him. Scared because no one had ever touched me there and excited because it was Benjamin. I wanted to be with him. In every way.

He pulled away and dug into his food, groaning at the taste. "You are cooking more often," he said, pointing his fork at me.

I grinned, secretly pleased that he was enjoying my cooking. I had never cooked much in the past; only when it was me and Mom when Johnny left for college.

We finished the rest of the meal in a comfortable silence with only talk about classes and the ink shop before he turned towards me.

"That was delicious." He wiped the corner of his mouth.

I grinned, raising my eyebrows. "I'm waiting," I teased.

"For what?" he asked, smirking at me. He knew what I was waiting for and it looked like he wanted me to wait a little longer.

I rolled my eyes, grabbed our plates and deposited them in the sink to rinse before I loaded them in the dishwasher. I looked back over my shoulder and saw that he was scrolling through his phone, probably checking his messages from the boys at work.

I walked over and cut a piece of fudge cake before sliding it in front of him with a spoon.

His eyes lit up as he looked up at me. He tilted his chin up and pressed his lips against mine before pulling back.

I chuckled as I went back to the sink, happy that the evening was going well. I was expecting a level of awkwardness or something but there was none. We worked well and I knew that everything over the last few months since Tillie moved to town had been for this. I was supposed to be right here with Benjamin.

This was where I belonged.

"What are you thinking about?" he asked, sneaking up behind me and wrapping his arms around my waist. "You look like you're a million miles away."

I turned in his arms and placed my hands on his chest before I looked up at him. "I'm not." I shook my head. "I'm right here where I belong."

I leaned forward and pressed my lips to his. I parted them and slid my tongue in to mingle with his. He tasted of chocolate and I wanted to taste every part of him.

He pulled back to look down at me. "Are you okay?"

I nodded before releasing a sigh. "Do you want me?" I asked. I felt vulnerable asking him this but I had to know... I had to know that he wanted me just as much as I wanted him.

"You know I do," he whispered. He looked confused as to why I was asking him this.

Benjamin had never hidden how much he wanted me—not even when we first got together. He'd always kissed me with the same reckless level of passion that I was only now starting to show him in return.

"Show me," I whispered. "Show me how much you want me."

He took a step back from me and my arms fell from around his shoulders. I thought he was rejecting me but then he held his hand out to me and I immediately took it, letting him lead me from the kitchen.

He kept hold of it until we got to the bedroom. He pulled me against him and placed my hands on his shoulders.

"For the last few months, you are all I have thought

about." He spoke those words with such truth and sincerity, it was impossible not to believe him. "I wanted this to be special. Perfect," he continued. "I wanted this to be a moment that you would always remember." He sighed and stroked my hair back from my face. "I wanted to be perfect for you."

"You are," I whispered. "I know it hasn't been easy," I continued, "but I'm happy that we got to where we are now." I looked into his beautiful green eyes. "I'm happy to be here with you."

"You really mean that," he stated.

I nodded and allowed him to push me down onto the bed. He crawled over me and touched his lips to mine before sucking my bottom lip into his. I groaned when he ran his tongue over it, feeling my cock harden in my pants.

He leaned back and grabbed the back of his shirt and pulled it up his body slowly.

My eyes zoned in on each patch of skin that was revealed. He lifted it up and off and let it drop to the floor. My eyes went to the lily tattoo that was on his chest near his heart. Her name was scrawled beneath surrounded by an infinity symbol.

He took my hands in his and placed them on his sides before he moved them up over his toned chest. My hands shook slightly and I knew it caught his attention from the way his grip tightened on my hands.

"It's okay," he whispered. "It's just me."

I smiled up at him, trying to show that I was okay. "I'm just nervous."

He nodded before he leaned back and stepped down off the bed. He held his hand out to me and I immediately took it, letting him pull me up. He wrapped his arm around my waist and pressed it against my lower back before he leaned his forehead down against mine.

"Are you sure you're ready for this?" he asked, staring into my eyes.

"I'm just tense," I whispered. I was ready for this. I wanted to be with Benjamin. I just wanted it to be perfect.

I wanted to be perfect for him.

He nodded before he pulled back and gazed down at me. "I'll go and turn the shower on." He leaned forward and kissed the corner of my mouth. "Come in when you're ready, okay?"

I nodded before he turned away and watched him walk out of the room. I took a seat down on the bed and rolled my shoulders, trying to work some of the tension out of my body.

Pull yourself together.

I heard the shower turn on and I waited for a few minutes. I stared across the room and chuckled when I saw a photo in a frame on top of his chest of drawers. I walked over and picked it up, grinning when I remembered taking the photo of Benjamin, Lily and myself.

I had gone to visit them at the shop and it was so quiet there that they'd been at her counter playing scrabble. I'd convinced them to close shop and we went to the bar they'd taken me to when I first met them. We'd taken several selfies before having a group one of the three of us goofing around and pulling silly faces.

I chuckled, remembering back to that day.

I set the photo back in its place and slipped my t-shirt off before toeing my shoes and socks off followed by my jeans and boxers. I was hard as a fucking rock and I knew that only one thing would ease this tension in my body.

I took a deep breath and followed the sound of the running water to the bathroom.

Benjamin was standing behind the condensed glass partition of his rather spacious shower cubicle with his head tilted back, letting the warm water run down over his body.

I slid the door open and stepped inside. As I closed it, he turned around slowly and placed his hands on my shoulders. My eyes trailed down to the tattoo on his upper arm of the band and star before coming back to his eyes.

"I'm sorry about that," I said, nodding my head back towards his bedroom.

"Don't worry about it." He pressed his fingers to my lips in a shushing motion. "Just be here with me. Let me love you."

I nodded and moved closer to him, letting him turn us so that I was fully beneath the spray. The warm water flowed down over my body, soaking into the tense muscles.

He reached up and slid the additional side sprays on and moments later, we were both soaked. He moved forward and pressed his lips to mine.

I closed my eyes and gave myself over to him, allowing him to lead.

His hands slid down over my sides and moved slowly towards where I was hard for him, his fingertips grazing over my wet flesh. He wrapped his hand around my shaft and moved his hand up and down.

I groaned against his lips, feeling myself grow harder against him.

His cock bobbed where it rested against my hip and I wanted nothing more than to taste him.

Would he like it? Would it turn him on having me my knees?

"I want to taste you," I whispered against his lips.

"Not tonight," he whispered, shaking his head. "Tonight is about you." He moved his hands off my cock and placed them on my hips. "Turn around," he whispered before sucking my earlobe in between his lips and nibbling on it.

I groaned, turning around, and faced the shower wall. He pressed himself against me from behind and began peppering kisses across the backs of my shoulders.

"Just relax," he whispered, "and focus on my touch."

I nodded, feeling the water run down over my muscles and his lips kiss across my shoulders.

Seconds later, he was moving his hand between my legs before his finger grazed up the crack of my ass.

I tensed on instinct, not prepared for the sensation it caused in me.

"It's okay," he whispered. He slid his finger against me before he eased it inside.

I groaned, my head hanging forward as he pressed his finger against me. I parted my legs instinctively, wanting him—wanting to help him in some way.

He eased his finger inside in small and short strokes. "You feel good, Sammy." He tilted his head and sucked my earlobe into his mouth. After a few strokes, he pulled his finger out and on the next stroke, he eased an additional finger inside me, opening me up. He was going slow, preparing me, but I wanted more.

I wanted him.

I tilted my hips back, easing his fingers deeper inside. I gasped at the strokes of pleasure that shot through me. It went straight to my cock, making me want him inside me desperately.

Logically I knew that two fingers were nowhere near enough but with every movement of his, it just made me want him more. I was hungry for him like I had never been for another.

"I want you," I whispered. I turned my head to the side, seeking his lips.

He pressed them against mine, roughly kissing me before pulling away and adding another finger.

"I need you ready for me."

I reached back and wrapped my hand around his cock. He was thick and hard. I knew it was going to hurt having him inside me but I had to have him. He was mine as much as I was his.

He took a step back, removing himself from my grasp. A few moments later, he slid his fingers free. He placed his hands on my hips before he kissed the arch of my shoulder.

"Are you ready for me, Sammy?"

I nodded my head. I was more than ready.

"Place your hands on the wall," he whispered, rubbing his thumbs back and forth over my hip bones.

I did as he said and waited. He removed his left hand and seconds later I felt his hardness against me.

"I'll go slow," he promised.

He eased forward and rubbed his cock against me. He slowly eased forward and I immediately tensed, my body not liking the intrusion.

"Relax, baby." He slid his other arm around me and took my cock in his hands. He began moving his hand up and down in long and firm strokes.

I groaned, closing my eyes and letting my head drop back against his shoulder. He held us both up and rotated his hips back and forth a few more times. His movements combined with the feel of his hand around my cock was making me come undone.

I rocked my hips back against him, moaning when I felt him slip further inside me.

He groaned in response. He slid out before sliding back in. "You feel so fucking good."

I groaned, moving back against him, levering my weight against the wall.

His hand moved up my chest before he tweaked my nipple, pulling and pinching.

I sucked in a breath, loving the feel of his lips on my neck. Kissing, sucking, nipping... marking me.

His hand sped up on my cock, squeezing the back of my cock. He was moving faster inside of me now. The only sounds in the room were the sound of us moving together and the spray falling down on us.

"I need you to come," he gasped, moving harder against me. "Come apart for me." He tightened his grip on my cock, twisting his wrist on the head before moving back down.

I groaned, feeling my balls begin to tighten. "I'm going to..." I shook my head against his shoulder, trying to warn him.

Seconds later, he slammed himself inside me.

We both called out each other's names as we came apart in each other's arms.

TWENTY-THREE

Benjamin

Lying in bed, I stared at the ceiling and tried to ignore the images that kept running through my mind. Being with Sammy was like nothing else... Being inside him, being the first to be with him in that way...

He was it for me. We'd yet to have that "I love you" moment but I knew he was happy with me.

I turned to look at his sleeping body next to me. He had the cutest pout on his face. It made me want to wake him up and do it all over again.

When we came back from our shower, Sammy had dried off and immediately climbed beneath the blanket. When I joined him, he'd shuffled his body over and laid his head on my chest.

I would never have pegged him as one, but my Sammy was a cuddler and I fucking loved it. I shook my head and looked back at the ceiling before closing my eyes, determined to ignore my throbbing cock and get some sleep.

Although, now that I had been inside, Sammy— now that I knew how he felt from the inside—it was all that I could fucking think about. Just as I was about to give up and climb out of bed to get a glass of water, the sheets shifted and Sammy rolled over, moving his warm body close to mine. He took my hand in his, entwining our fingers.

"You're restless," he whispered. He looked up at me looking worried. "Is everything okay?"

"I can't sleep." I raised my arm and slid it beneath him, loving the way he cuddled closer into my warmth. "Too wired, I guess."

He nodded and laid his head back down, wrapping his arm around me and placing it on my hip. My cock jumped at the contact but I ignored it, trying to relax my body and fall into a blissful sleep.

After a few moments of silence, Sammy tilted his head and pressed small kisses against my neck. It was very distracting. It was not helping me to stay relaxed. It was making me fucking harder and getting me more revved up. Without warning, Sammy moved forward and slid his leg over me. He leaned his weight down on his knees and hands on either side of my body.

"W-what are you doing?" I asked, stammering.

He smirked down at me, the light from outside the window reflecting on his body.

"I want you," he whispered. He moved his face closer to mine and rubbed the end of his nose against mine before giving me a sweet kiss.

"We can't," I whispered, shaking my head. "You'll be too sore."

Fucking him twice in one night was not an option. I wasn't exactly on the small side and Sammy had already taken more of me inside him on our first time than I had anticipated. No way was it happening again tonight.

His eyes trailed down to my chest. He was thinking and I could see when the realization started to sink in. The cutest little frown appeared on his face before a devious little smile began to appear on his face.

"What about you?" he asked. He trailed a pointer finger down the center of my chest and it took everything in me to ignore it.

He was trying to wrap me around his little finger. The pathetic thing was that I had been wrapped around that little finger of his ever since he walked into my fucking life. He had to know that by now.

"What about me?" I asked, looking up at him.

He smiled at me before leaning down and licking the side of my lip, sucking and nibbling his way up to my ear. Sammy was very good with his mouth.

His breath blew against my ear before he whispered, "What if I fuck you?"

I could have come right then from hearing Sammy talk about fucking me. Was I ready to have Sammy inside of me?

Fuck, yes, I was.

"Is that something you would like?" he asked, pulling back until he was kneeling over me.

I could hear the desperation start to creep into his voice and it fucking pissed me off. I thought we were done with this hesitation bullshit. Didn't he know how much he fucking owned me?

I reached up and grasped the back of his head and yanked his lips down to mine. "Yes!" I growled against his lips. I thrust my tongue into his mouth and groaned as he pushed his weight down on me. His cock rubbed against my stomach. The feel of him hard against me was too much. I pulled away, needing him too much.

"You're going to need lube," I whispered. I nodded my head towards the chest of drawers. Before I could move to get it, Sammy was already on his feet and opening the top drawer. He turned and walked back towards me with the small bottle and two condoms in his hand.

"You'll have to direct me." He chuckled, handing me the bottle and a condom.

Fuck, this was turning me on way more than it should.

I parted my legs and patted the mattress in between them. I wasn't going to last long with Sammy inside of me.

He climbed onto the bed and kneeled in between my parted legs. We were both rock hard and I knew this was going to be different. So fucking different than any other time I had ever been with another man.

I quickly tore the condom open and moved it down on my length, groaning when I moved my hand up and down several times. I took the condom out of Sammy's hand and leaned forward. Taking his cock in my hand, I jerked him up and down a few times before placing the condom over his head and sliding it down over his thick shaft.

He moaned, his hips shifting forward for more. "That felt good," he whispered.

I restrained myself from teasing him how much better it would feel when he was inside of me. I didn't think I could handle it if Sammy started talking about fucking me.

I squeezed some lube into my hands before taking his cock in my hand again and rubbing my hand up and down. He groaned, his head dropping back at the contact.

Fuck, he was beautiful.

I added a little more, not wanting him to worry or struggle. I just needed him inside me.

I lay back, watching him kneel in between my legs. I held my arms out to him and he came straight to me. I tilted my hips up, trying to align myself with him so that he didn't have to fumble too much.

He raised his eyebrows, silently asking my permission.

I nodded, moaning against his lips when he kissed me.

He leaned back on his knees and pushed forward. The head of his cock touched where I needed him. I groaned at the friction, realizing how long it had been since I had been with anyone. I was desperate for him.

He pushed forward, his head slowly moving inside me. He began repeating my movements from earlier and pressed forward before moving back, rocking his hips in slow and steady strokes.

I moaned, the sight of him above me making me

crazy. I parted my legs a little more, hoping to help him.

He groaned, moving his hips further inside. "You feel really good." He sounded a little awestruck.

"I need you inside," I whispered. "It's okay." I nodded my head, silently telling him that I could take it. I could take him all.

He nodded and slowly moved forward until I felt his balls rest against me.

"Fuck!" he gasped. He moved his hands forward and took my hips before pulling back.

"Yes," I moaned. I reached up and placed my hands on his chest, needing to feel his skin.

He groaned and pushed back in, his speed picking up a little. He broke our gaze before he looked down to where we were joined.

"Ah, fuck," he whispered before pulling back. On the next pass, he slammed back inside of me.

I moaned, feeling my muscles squeeze him. "You like that," I whispered. "You like fucking me."

"Fuck, I do." He leaned down and roughly pressed his lips to mine.

My hands slid down off his chest at the change of position.

Fuck, he felt so good inside of me. I moved my hand to grasp his shoulder and trailed the other down to his ass. I grabbed his ass cheek and pulled him against me.

"Fuck me harder," I whispered. "I want to feel you tomorrow."

He groaned, lifting his hips back and slamming back inside of me. "Like that?" he asked.

That was fucking rhetorical. He kept up his rhythm, fucking me with that magnificent cock of his.

"You feel good," he whispered. "Your ass is squeezing my cock."

Fuck, Sammy was a talker.

"I love fucking you." He panted, sweat forming on his chest as he fucked me into the mattress. "Seeing you beneath me, knowing that it's me doing this to you..."

I moaned, feeling my balls begin to tighten. I reached down and took my cock in my grasp, stroking my hands up and down roughly.

He slammed his hips forward, the sound of his balls slapping against me.

"Squeeze me," he gasped. "I need to come."

I tightened my grip before he reached down and took my nipple in between his finger and thumb.

"Come apart for me, darling," he whispered, using my hips to slam me down against him. "I want to hear you."

I moaned, coming apart for him. I filled the condom at the same time that he slammed himself back inside me before collapsing down on my chest.

"Fuck," he gasped. He turned his head and laid it down on my chest.

I chuckled and wrapped my arms around him, feeling him soften inside of me. "You okay?" I smoothed his hair back before kissing the top of his hair.

"Fucking amazing!" He grinned and leaned up, kissing me on the lips quickly.

He stood up and walked towards the bathroom in all his glory.

If you had told me several weeks ago that Sammy and I would be this happy, I would have told you that you were fucking crazy but right now...

I was happy. We were happy.

I slid the condom off and tied a knot in it before disposing of it in the bin by the side of the bed. I pulled the blankets back over me just as Sammy came back into the bedroom.

I held my arm out to him and he immediately curled his body against me, resting his head on my chest. I had never been a cuddler before but with Sammy, I now fucking loved cuddle time.

We lay in peaceful silence and I finally felt my body

start to relax. The gentle pitter-patter sound of rain-drops hitting the glass window was putting me into a peaceful state.

Sammy stirred at my side as he cuddled himself closer. Several moments later, I heard the most beautiful sound in the world.

"I love you, Benjamin."

I snapped my head down to him, shocked that I was hearing it. Shocked that he was actually saying it to me. I opened my mouth to say something before closing it. I must have looked like a demented goldfish before he giggled.

"I'm in love with you," he whispered. He slid his arm up and over my chest and placed it over my heart. "I love you and only you."

I leaned down at the same time as he leaned up and pressed my lips to his. We both smiled against each other's mouth like a couple of crazy freaks before leaning into the kiss again.

"I love you too, Sammy," I whispered. "I've always loved you."

He held himself tighter to me and placed his head on my chest before entwining our legs where we stayed until sunrise, still wrapped in each other, in our own sweet bubble of happiness.

TWENTY-FOUR

Benjamin

Several weeks had gone by since the day that Sammy and I first made love. It had brought us closer since that day: physically and emotionally.

Being with him was simple. It was easy—just like breathing. It just came naturally to us. If we were in public, Sammy would often reach for my hand. Just the smallest touch would be more than enough of us. We didn't throw it in people's faces that we were together but we didn't hide it either.

Sammy spent most of his days here lately. My once very clean apartment was now littered with notepads and study books. He usually set up in the kitchen to study but more often than not, we'd often spend our evenings on the sofa.

We'd fall into a comfortable routine. When he'd be busy focusing on his essays, I would usually be sketching my ideas down for new art pieces. We had begun posting new pieces on our website and social media pages for ideas for any willing customers and it had boosted our number of walk-in customers.

We divided the rest of our time between spending time with his family and mine and occasionally I would join them at the arena for Johnny's games. We were all prepared for Sammy to get low but it never happened. He always looked very proud watching his brother play.

Sammy was a beautiful soul inside and out and I was lucky that my path had led me to him.

"I can't do this fucking thing," I mumbled, staring at my reflection in Johnny's hallway.

I twisted the knot in my hands before undoing it and yanking it off. I froze when I heard a giggle come from behind me. I rolled my eyes and turned around, coming face to face with Tillie.

"Tillie..." I was dumbstruck. "You look absolutely gorgeous."

She was dressed in a beautiful black dress. It had capped sleeves and came down to her ankles. Her gold jigsaw piece was glistening on a chain around her neck and her hair was pinned back with gentle waves trailing over her shoulders.

"Thank you." She blushed at the compliment before she took a step toward me. "Would you like some help?"

"Please." I held the black tie out to her and tilted my chin.

"You can't exactly go to a formal event without a black tie now, can you?" she asked rhetorically. She smiled up at me, her eyes twinkling.

"I don't know why I'm coming," I chuckled. "It's a team event and I'm not on the team."

She grinned up at me, her sparkly white teeth on full display. "That's true," she said, wrapping the material over and beginning to form the knot. "But you are family."

I smiled down at her, nodding my head. "Yeah, I guess so."

"And besides," she said, tucking the end of the tie through the loop and pulling it down. "Tonight will be special." She tightened the knot before smoothing it down.

"Special how?" I asked, confused. "I thought tonight was to honor the coach for being with the team for thirty years."

Her eyes twinkled up at me. "That's special, right?"

I knew mischief when I saw it, and Tillie was definitely being mischievous. She had a secret about tonight.

I watched her walk out to the kitchen where Johnny was leaning against the worktop in the kitchen. She went straight to him, his arms wrapping around her waist. He pressed his lips to her forehead before reaching his hand up and playing with the end of her curls.

I had learned from being around Tillie and Johnny that words weren't necessary. They often shared what they were thinking with the smallest of touches. Watching them, you couldn't help but believe in love. With them, it was real.

I turned around when I heard movement behind me. There Sammy stood, looking very fuckable in his navy suit.

"There you are." He walked over and gave me a quick kiss on the lips. "You look very handsome." He smiled at me before Logan walked in.

Johnny and Tillie joined us in the living room before they led us to the front door. Johnny was holding Tillie's hand in his, paying extra attention to the ring on her finger. It made me wonder when they planned on tieing the knot.

After a short walk, we arrived at the conference center. It was a new building in town, and it was used quite regularly by large corporations. The college had obviously rented it out for the evening.

I looked around when we entered the hall, surprised at how many people were there. Judging by the look on Sammy's face, I wasn't the only one that was surprised by the number.

We followed Johnny over to the table before he took Sammy and Logan to a long table of faculty members. They stopped in front of an older gentleman who I assumed was the coach.

"That's the coach," Tillie said, taking a seat in front of her place card.

I took the seat allocated for me, leaving a seat in between her and Sammy. I peeked at the place card next to me and smiled when I saw it had Bex's name on there. "There are a lot of non-team people here," I said, hoping she'd pick up on the hint.

Was football seriously that popular here that everyone wanted to celebrate the coach? Surely I was missing something here.

She grinned before taking a sip of her water and avoiding my question completely.

"What's up, losers?" Bex teased, arriving at the

table. She bent down and gave me a kiss on the cheek before moving around the table and giving Tillie a hug. "Does he know yet?" she asked quietly.

"Does who know what?" I asked, trying to get in on the conversation.

Something was going on and I was completely out of the loop.

"Nothing," they both said, their voices sounding extra chirpy. They had sweet smiles on their faces but I wasn't buying it.

Sammy and Johnny started to walk back towards us and Bex and Sammy took their seats, sandwiching me in between them. Sammy put his hand on my leg and I instantly covered it with mine, needing the contact.

I could feel several sets of eyes on us but I ignored them. It didn't matter that they were staring. It didn't seem to be bothering Sammy either, so I shrugged it off, determined to try and relax and enjoy the night.

Minutes later, the waiters were bringing orders of drinks that everyone had placed at the bar. I'd opted for a beer, needing my inhibitions to loosen up a little.

After dinner, several people were served for chocolate mousse. The waiter brought Tillie hers and she enthusiastically dug in. It was a little awkward when Johnny stared at her mouth every time she licked the spoon but I tried to ignore it. No guesses as to what they would be doing when they got home later.

Probably the same thing I'd be doing to Sammy when we got back to mine.

I shook my head, trying to rid the thoughts of fucking Sammy. Getting hard at a dinner table with his family wouldn't exactly be the greatest thing to do.

The music slowly died down before Chunk got out of his seat. He made his way to the podium and patted the coach comfortingly on his shoulder as he passed him, smiles being exchanged between them both.

I looked over at Tillie and wondered what was going on before she gave me a cheeky wink and placed her hand on Johnny's hand, resting on the table.

"Good evening, ladies and gentleman," he said into the microphone. His voice was strong and clear and I could see why he was the captain of this team. He was a leader. It showed in his voice and physical presence. He looked over the audience, his eyes briefly landing on Johnny before he looked away.

"I'm honored to stand up here and present a very special award. We are all here tonight to celebrate with our coach and support his tremendous achievements in the sporting sector." He smiled over at the coach before he looked back towards the back of the hall.

"Although, first," he continued, "I am here to introduce someone else. Another award is going to be given tonight. Please welcome Johnny Baker."

Sammy looked over at his brother in shock before the entire room erupted into applause.

"Thank you," he said, swapping places with Chunk.

I watched as Chunk came back and took his seat next to Bex. He gave her a small wink before turning back to look at Johnny.

"So, I am here to present a very special award: the MVP—most valuable player." He smiled, waving his hand to the coach. "A couple of weeks ago, Coach called a team meeting and discussed who he thought should be presented with this very special award."

I looked over at Tillie and smiled when I saw how proud she looked. She had tears pooled in her eyes, watching Johnny stand up there.

"We all agreed—the entire team—that this person deserves this award." He cleared his throat before continuing. "So first of all, what is a player? What makes a person the MVP? He grinned and looked over at Tillie, his smile stretching when he looked at her. "An MVP is someone who puts themselves before the line. Someone who will do whatever it takes to get the job done and get the team through difficulties and struggles." He leaned his hands on the podium, his stance looking forceful and strong. "This team..." He looked around the room and made eye contact with several members that were spread through the room. "This team is a family—every single one of us."

Sammy smiled before reaching over and taking my hand in his.

"The person that is receiving this award has done just that. They laid everything on the line to step up and be their own person. Even if that meant stepping out of the line and saying 'this is me'."

I looked over at Tillie and it was all clicking into place. She nodded and we both looked back at Johnny.

"This individual laid not only his position on this team on the line but he also laid his life down."

Sammy tensed and I knew he was starting to realize what tonight was all about.

The coach looked over at him and smiled; he looked so proud of Sammy and I knew that every single person in this room felt the same.

"Several months ago, an intruder broke into my home and was armed with a gun." He paused and looked over at us. "This person aimed a gun at me and pulled the trigger."

Sammy looked anxious. He hated the spotlight and he knew that he would have to get up.

I couldn't have been prouder of him at this moment.

"This person saved my life, the life of my fiancé and is the reason I am standing here today." He paused for a few moments and I knew that Johnny was close to tears. "Please welcome to the stage my baby brother, Sammy Baker. This team's most valuable player."

We all stood and Sammy tightened his grip on my hand before he turned to Tillie. She wrapped her arms tightly around him, the tears now streaming down over her cheeks.

"Thank you, Sammy," she whispered, giving him a kiss on his cheek before releasing him from the hug.

Sammy moved past her, grinning when Logan gave him a supportive pat on the back.

The sound of the applause was roaring and I was so proud of him to have this huge community behind him.

The coach was now standing at the podium with a glass plaque in his hand. He shook Sammy's hand, smiling proudly at him. They exchanged a few quiet words before Sammy moved past him and came face to face with Johnny.

They stepped up to each other and wrapped their arms around each other, squeezing each other tightly. Johnny reached up and patted Sammy on the back of his head before he stepped down from the podium and made his way back to his seat by Tillie.

The applause continued for a few moments before it slowly died down and everyone took their seats.

The coach handed Sammy his award before moving back to his seat.

"Thank you so much, guys." Sammy chuckled into the microphone, looking a little awestruck. "I, uh, I don't really know what to say..."

Several members of the audience laughed.

"Family. What can I say about family, huh?" He grinned, looking around the room before continuing. "The last few months haven't been the easiest."

His eyes went to Tillie and I knew that what he had given, what he had sacrificed, had been a large price to pay. But he had never complained about it.

"No family is perfect. We may argue, fight, scream and yell, but it doesn't change anything. There is no line when it comes to family and I am honored to have an amazing one." He raised the award, still looking a little shocked. "Thank you so much for this wonderful parting gift and I will never forget it. Thank you." He nodded his head a final time before he stepped back and made his way back to the table.

I smiled over at him and took his hand in mine. He was shaking and I knew this award had hit home just how special and important he was to every single person sat at this table.

Sammy was special and I would never get tired of reminding him just how much.

A few hours had passed since Sammy had received the MVP award. We had walked home to my apartment where he had placed the award on the coffee table and had been staring at it ever since.

I took a seat next to him and laid my arm across the back of the sofa behind him.

Moments later, he angled his body towards me and laid his head on my chest.

I slid my arm around him and held him close to me, comforting him.

"Are you okay, Sammy?" I asked, resting my chin on the top of his head.

He inhaled a shaky breath before nodding. "I'm okay. I just didn't expect that."

"They wanted to show how much they appreciated you."

He nodded and wrapped his arm around my waist. "it was special," he whispered.

I nodded, considering my next words. I had been

planning to ask him an important question tonight but now I wasn't so sure.

Maybe I should wait. It might be too soon for this. For him.

"What is it?" he asked, tilting his head up to look at me. "I can tell when you have something you want to talk to me about."

I chuckled, realizing he knew me better than I knew myself most days. "It's nothing." I shook my head, hoping he would drop it.

"It's something if it's bothering you." His words sounded so genuine.

"I, uh..." I sighed, trying to find the nerve. "Okay I, uh..."

"You're stammering," he commented. "Just say it. it's just me."

I nodded. "There's no wrong answer to this question but I... I was wondering if you wanted to move in with me."

He froze, obviously not expecting it. His eyes flicked down to my chest before he looked back up at me several moments later.

"I would love to," he whispered. He slid his hand up my arm and placed his hand on the back of my head before pulling my lips down to his.

TWENTY-FIVE

Sammy

Several weeks passed before I even started thinking about moving my stuff over. My class load had doubled on the build-up towards the end of the year and I knew it was only a taste of what was to come.

When we told the gang that I was moving in with Benjamin, I had expected problems. Maybe some arguments. I hadn't been with Benjamin long term exactly but our relationship was built on a stronger foundation, in my eyes. Benjamin had been there for me from the start and had been a solid wall for me to fall back on.

It was time to now build us up together as one.

"It looks so empty in here," Tillie's voice echoed from the doorway

I turned around and immediately held my arms out to her.

She smiled, rolling her eyes at herself before she stepped forward and wrapped her arms around me, cuddling into my chest.

"Don't miss me too much," I teased.

She dug her finger into my ribs and cuddled herself closer. "Don't even joke about that. You're leaving me with two football addicts. Who's going to keep me company now when they start talking statistics!"

I chuckled. *Who knew Tillie Jacobs was dramatic?*

"I'm not going far," I whispered. "I'm only around the corner." I kissed her forehead, inhaling her strawberry scent. "I'll still see you every day."

She nodded before pulling away and pointed to the last item on my very empty desk. "Don't forget that." She grinned and walked away, leaving me alone again.

I walked over and picked it up, grinning at how goofy we all looked. It was a photo of the three of us—Johnny, Logan and myself—all huddled together while Tillie took the photo. She had insisted that we should all capture more photos of us all together to look back on one day.

I slid it into my backpack before lifting it on to my back and jogging down the stairs. At the same time,

Johnny and Logan came back in followed by Benjamin.

"That's the last of it," Johnny declared. He slid his arm around Tillie's shoulders, rolling his eyes mockingly at me over her head.

"I'll see you losers later," Logan said, clapping me on the shoulder. "See you later, bro."

I chuckled at his easy going nature. Nothing fazed that man.

"I guess I'll see you guys later, then."

Benjamin stepped forward until he was next to me. "You guys are welcome at any time."

Johnny held his hand out to Benjamin and they shook hands. They had become close over the last few weeks and I was happy to see that. I looked down at Tillie and frowned when I saw her biting down hard on her bottom lip.

"Tillie..."

Before I could even open my arms to her, she lunged forward and crushed me in a tight hug.

Then came the sobs...

Whenever Tillie got emotional or anxious, she would do this strange hiccup sob thing. I hated that my moving out was having this effect on her, but she was acting like I was moving halfway across the world instead of just around the corner.

"I'm going to see you every day," I said, trying to soothe her. I rubbed my hand up and down her back. "You'll get sick of seeing me."

She turned her face sideways and rested her cheek against my chest. "But who's going to watch Disney movies or with me?" She sucked in a breath before continuing. "O-or sit with me when I sketch." Another hiccup. "And brush my hair for me when it gets wet."

I chuckled, looking at Johnny behind her. "I'm sure Johnny is happy to do all that for you."

He grinned, crossing his arms.

"And as for the Disney stuff, I don't think Benjamin has ever seen a Disney movie."

She looked over at him, eyeing him like he was crazy.

"It's true." He shrugged non-commitally. "Never seen a Disney movie."

She pulled back and wiped beneath her eyes. "Well, that's just awful." She eyed him again before continuing. "Maybe I can come over and we can start the classics."

Benjamin grinned before nodding his head. "I'd really like that, Tillie."

She smiled warmly at him before stepping back, leaning against Johnny's chest.

"I feel a little better now."

We all chuckled at her emotional state before turning around and walking out the door and making our way across the road to Joy's. She had invited myself and Benjamin over with the promise of having something special waiting for us.

I was really hoping it was cookies.

I led Benjamin through the path of her garden, knocking on her porch door.

"Come on in, sweet boys," her voice rang out.

I stepped inside, following the gorgeous smell of baking to the kitchen where Joy was sitting with a plate of cookies waiting and three cups of hot chocolate.

"Hope you don't mind staying to have a cup of tea with this old lady," she teased, winking at Benjamin.

I chuckled, leaning down and giving her a kiss on her cheek.

"You all packed?" she asked.

I nodded and stole a cookie before Benjamin could. "Logan and Johnny helped to move it all

"They are good boys," she said, praising them.

I stared at her. "Are you okay?" I asked. "I'm sorry I haven't been over a lot lately."

"Don't be silly." She waved her hand dismissively. "You kids are busy with work and classes."

"We'll be over more," I promised. I hated the

thought of her being on her own so much. "What happened to that mister of yours?" I winked at her, trying to get a laugh.

"He moved to be closer to his family. They had their first grandchild." She looked so happy for him.

I nodded my head and listened as she turned the conversation to Benjamin and his shop. She had never been into an ink shop before. He had promised her a tour in a few weeks when her workload with the church and hospital died down.

An hour later, we were leaving Joy's loaded up with way too many cookies: she hadn't taken no for an answer. She had also snuck a fresh fudge cake into the packages for Benjamin.

That woman was a rockstar in the kitchen.

As we arrived home, I smiled when I saw how much of a mess his place was. He had ink magazines all over the place and my textbooks were now starting to look like a tower piled high on the coffee table.

I walked over towards the window, watching the traffic move down below.

I smiled, closing my eyes when I felt Benjamin's chest press against my back. I leaned back, inhaling his clean scent of peppermint.

"Are you okay?" he asked before pressing a kiss to the side of my head.

I closed my eyes, letting that beautiful feeling travel through me.

"I'm better than okay," I whispered. "I'm happy. So happy."

I placed my hands over his as they wrapped around my waist, loving the feeling that traveled through me.

We were perfect.

Perfect and now complete.

Acknowledgments

I'd like to thank you for reading this book. I hope you have enjoyed it!

I would also like to thank these amazing women – Kathryn Dee, Rebecca Barber, Jade Pitman, Julie Tinkler, Scarlett Redd, Tracy Anne Wood, Scarlet Le Clair & Emma Lloyd – your support and belief in me has been amazing and I'm so thankful to everything you've done for me. From the daily pimping to all the support I receive from you. It means more to me than you know.

To my beta readers – Kathryn Dee, Rebecca Barber, Lorren Smith, Paula Tarpley Genereau, Amanda Williams, Kathryn Stokes & Emma Lloyd – thank you all so much for your honesty and support.

To my mother, Susan, again, thank you again for just being the best mother.

To Carl and Stuart, my brothers. Thanks for just being there (and often making fun of me lol).

Eleanor Lloyd-Jones. Thank you for being my editor!

And last, but certainly not least, thank you to all the amazing bloggers that have helped me. What you do for the author community is amazing and authors would be lost without you.

Hope you enjoy this book and love Sammy & Benjamin as much as I do!

Love,

Lizzie x

Also by Lizzie James

Kindred Series

Missing Piece

Perfect Fit

Rough Love

Tangled Series

Tangled Web

Tangled Lies

Tangled Truths: A Tangled/Kindred Crossover

Tangled Pieces

Winter's Rose Duet

Safe With You

Live For Me

Standalones

Gravity Happens

Shared World Novels

Confessions of a Troubled Rebel: A FratHouse Confessions Novel

Devastated by Fire: A Firehouse 13 Novel

Lost in Between Series

(Co-written with C.N. Marie)

The Lies of Gravity

The Sins of Silence

The Ink of Denial

Printed in Great Britain
by Amazon